MAXIMIZING LIFE'S OPPORTUNITIES

Exploring the Principles of a Purposeful Living

*Preparation is essential to create a positive experience
for a new day or the New Year.*

Dr. Moses O. Adedipe

REVISED EDITION

MERCYLAND
PUBLISHING HOUSE

Maximizing Life's Opportunities
Exploring the Principles of Purposeful Living
Revised Edition: April 2023
Printed in the United States of America.

ISBN - Paperback: 978-0-9786637-3-5
Mercyland Publishing House (MPH)
Mercyland Inc (www.mercylandinc.com)

Revised by: Dr. Daniel Olulana (CEO Fotur Global Media), Pastor Austin Ameh, Abe Opeyemi, and Akinruli Paul

Design & Compiled by: Akinruli Paul
www.paulcyber.com.ng

Contact Information:
Camp Of God Family

281-804-2520, 281-324-0060
https://www.campofgod.com
info@camofgod.org
mosesadedipe.com
info@mosesadedipe.com
Arewamose@gmail.com

TABLE OF CONTENTS

Acknowledgment

I give all the glory, honor, and adoration to the Lord Jesus Christ, my Saviour, my Helper, my Defender, my Sustainer for His mercies, blessings, and also yet another great opportunity given to me to write this book. If it had not been the "**I AM THAT I AM**" in my life, I would have been messed up by the powers and principalities of darkness; I would have been dead and forgotten long ago. Jesus, my Lord, and Master, I owe you, my life.

Let me acknowledge before God and man, how fortunate I am to have met my sweetheart, my wife, Catherine, "*Arewa*", who is the best thing that has ever happened to me. My wife is the best divine favour I have received from the Lord. The truth is that it takes a special woman to marry a man like me. So, I thank God that He hand-selected "*Arewa*" to be my partner and to walk this journey of life with me. I thank God, every day, for giving me a wife like her. God has used her tremendously in my personal life and ministry. I cannot thank her enough; only

God can reward her for all her labours and support in Jesus' name.

To the Zero Hour Family of *"Prayer, Power, Praise, and Purpose"* at Christ Apostolic Church Revival Center, Houston, Texas, I acknowledge your love and support; you are the best and I am so proud of you all. Always remember, the bottom is too crowded, the middle is tight, and the only option is above. God, almighty, bless you in Jesus' name. I love you all.

My sincere appreciation goes to my siblings, namely: Evangelist Arikeola Olubusoye, Mr. Fatai Lawal and his wife (Evangelist Elizabeth Lawal), Evangelist Victoria Adedipe, Pastor Peter and his wife (Evangelist Mary Akinyanju). I will never forget you, my only brother, Pastor Adeyinka Adedipe. Jesus has made you the rock of our family. We can't wait to see your face again. Thank you for your prayer and support.

To all men and women of God, who have contributed positively to my success in the ministry: Pastor (Dr.) EHL Olusheye, Prophet (Dr.) S.K Abiara, Pastor (Dr.) Bayo Ijelu and the entire Basiribasiri Prayer Ministry team in Akure, Pastor (Dr.) Joshua Owoeye, Pastor (Dr.) David Adenodi, Pastor (Dr.) Timothy Agbeja, Pastor (Dr.) S.O Oladele, Pastor (Dr.) Famuyide, Pastor (Dr.) S. O Akinsulure, Pastor (Dr.) Kola Sonaike, Pastor (Dr.) Abi Olowe, Pastor (Dr.) Tai Olamigoke of RCCG, House of David, Pastor Isaac Abiara, Pastor Z.O Oloba, Pastor Yemi Ayeni, Pastor

Tunji Ayeni, Pastor Christie Ogbeide, Pastor Babatunde Osho, Pastor Akinyanju, Pastor Olorunesan Bankola, Pastor Akin Ogunsusi and, of course, my special friend, Pastor Edmond Gbenebichie and his wife. Thank you all for your prayer, support, and encouragement.

To my four children who have made parenting easy and interesting; they are my special "4T" Tolulope, Temilola, Temitope, and Temilayo. You are the best and I love you all so much. My Father in Heaven who gave you all to us will watch over you in Jesus' name. Amen.

Dr. Moses O. Adedipe
Founder, Camp of God Ministry

Foreword

There is a famous saying, "Opportunity comes and goes; once it's gone, it may not come back in a lifetime."

This book is written in a simple, yet concise way for the reader to understand all about the opportunities we have been given to work for our Creator, fulfill our divine assignments, and the opportunity to truly accept or realign our lives with Jesus as our personal Lord and Saviour.

There are many ministry opportunities such as: going on a mission, organizing free Medical care services, feeding the poor, and clothing the naked. Yet, the greatest opportunity is, making ourselves available, to reach the unreached and touch the untouched. Someone out there needs to be reached.

This book helps us to understand how to overcome procrastination, plan our finances very well, respect time, and so on. Every step needed to make great changes in our lives so that we can do exploits for God and thereby become pleasing unto Him is also outlined!

It is what we do for Christ that lasts. Therefore, let us take advantage of the opportunities we have today and do something good for someone because the time is short and the night is coming when no one can work. We will give an account of our activities in due time before God.

Haven read through this book, "Making The Most of Every Opportunity," and I highly recommend it to all. It will change your life. It will challenge and encourage you. I was blessed by it. More Grace and anointing to you, Pastor Moses Adedipe!

Pastor Tai Olamigoke
Redeemed Christian Church of God
- House of David, Houston, Texas.

Information to Bring Changes in Any Life!

The book is relevant, easy to understand, and straight to the point. It contains a lot of real-life examples that make the contents applicable to all. I strongly recommend the book to all those who seek to manage their time better, run their lives easier, and live each day in the realization that they are operating within the realms of God's will and guidance.

Pastor Kolawole Sonaike
Superintendent, Texas Zone,
Christ Apostolic Church, Houston Texas

A Timely Book for This Season

This book communicates the right word for this season as everyone is seeking to know how to bring a change in his/her life. Within these pages lies the answer to man's ever-present problem of achieving success; step by step. This book is inspired by God and I pray that all who read it will allow their spirit to take in the information and put it to use to change their lives and thereby go out and do exploits for God. The creation is waiting for the manifestation of the sons of God; those who will change the world through their faith and actions.

Olabisi Odubanjo-Owen
- Elohim House
World Evangelism Outreach Ministries

Preface

A year has gone and another has rolled in again. The unfortunate reality about this is that we make resolutions for every year but only watch the year-end with our resolutions still on paper. Here comes a New Year; yet the lives of most people remain the same, with no change realized from all their years of wishing and planning for change. Everyone looks forward to the New Year, but little or no preparation is usually made to make it a different and positive one from the experience of the previous year.

Many, towards the end of the year, make repeated New Year resolutions that never see the light of the day because these resolutions are all mostly forgotten as soon as they are made. The point to note is that entering the New Year is not as important as really making the year a New Year. In the same vein, we need to resolve the question of what will make the year a new and different year. Will it be a function of the number of days, the hours of the day, the weeks of the month, or the months of the year? Of course not! How then can the Year be a New and different Year? Could it be that this year will be just another opportunity to go through January to December doing the same things again? Is it going to be another opportunity to make broken promises and resolutions again? Could it be another daily, weekly, or monthly routine that usually yields nothing but frustration and sadness?

If you are **25 or 75 years** old today, it implies also that you will have witnessed the same number of New Year celebrations on earth, either passively or actively. Unfortunately, the time in each day counted in these past years has only been spent doing the same thing, in all respects. If you observe, you will realize that you have only been living a routine life of sleeping, waking, eating, going to work, and paying bills, without making any other tangible achievement all the while.

When I sought the face of God for this year and while reflecting on my own life, the Lord gave me a very unique and unusual message. He said, "Your faith, your fear, your mindset, your courage, the power of your word, and how you make the most of the opportunity that I, the Lord, give you in the land of the living, will determine your success or your failure".

Honestly, you are what you say and what you think. Your destiny is the complete sum total of all your words, faith, thoughts, and fear. Everything in life starts with faith and is expressed through the words of your mouth.

> *"And God said, "Let there be light and there was light"*
> **Genesis 1:3**

Here, we see a good example of God's faith in action while He spoke. His words demonstrated Faith. First, God imagined in His heart what He wanted to create, and then He spoke it into existence with His Word by faith, knowing that His Word carries the power to create. Faith expressed by the spoken Word was the invisible force behind the creation of heaven and the earth, even before their actual physical manifestation. God, Himself, is the Word and the force behind what He says emanates from Him to make the invisible become visible.

> *"God, who gives life to the dead and calls those things which do not exist as though they did…"*
> **Roman 4:17b**

Faith sees the end result before the beginning of the journey; faith imagines and creates things from the invisible, making them visible. Fear works similarly: fear sees failure; it creates failure from the invisible, causing it to look real in the visible; fear tells you that you cannot do it, but faith says, with God all things are possible.

> *"I can do all this through him who gives me strength."*
> **Philippian 4:13**

Fear drives success completely out of your life while faith in your heart empowers you to succeed. If, for any reason, you allow fear to operate in your life, it will destroy your destiny and ground you to a halt, just like it did last year (regardless of resolutions). Let me ask you this question: when last did fear to empower or encourage you to accomplish anything great in the last **20 years** of your life? You will remember that every successful journey of yours in the past years was because you took bold steps of faith and God backed you up. Why are you afraid to make changes? Why do you believe the fake shreds of evidence created by fear that appears to be real?

Remember that, your thoughts and your feelings influence your decision, which turns out to become your actions and your actions form your habit while your habit makes up your character and your character affects your destiny.

I believe that you have made your New Year resolution as usual, and you have promised God hundreds of things. You must have also asked and claimed four thousand of His promises according to the word of the Scriptures. I know right now you are fired up and ready to conquer mountains and possess the land from this month until the end of the year, but in reality, the sun still rises and sets the same way in your life; the water flows, the air blows, the birds fly, you eat, drink, sleep and wake up still the same way. Nothing seems to be changing about you and yet, regardless of living a monotonous life, we are moving closer to our grave every second. There is nothing mankind can do to stop death when it shows up; the only antidote is Jesus Christ.

It is time we faced the reality that, none of us is growing younger and we are moving closer to our graves with every second that passes. How then can you make the most of the opportunity set before you by God before death knocks on your door? This is what should bother your mind the most.

We've got to realize the fact that we are privileged to be alive and we only have one life to live.

My focus in this book is, to help you reflect on your past, ponder on your present situations and then make better decisions about your future. I will share with you the secret of success; the key ingredient to having your prayers answered and, finally, teach you how to make the most of the God-given opportunities for you this year.

Maximizing Life's Opportunities

Exploring the Principles of a Purposeful Living

Ephesians 5:15-16 (AMP)

[15] " Look carefully then how you walk! Live purposefully and worthily and accurately, not as the unwise and witless, but as wise (sensible, intelligent people),
[16] Making the very most of the time [buying up each opportunity], because the days are evil."

Chapter 1

Faith Determines "Destiny"

It is astonishing, yet sad, to discover that, for many people,
the New Year will be a continuation of the past year.

Aside from the change of calendar from last year to the New Year, nothing new seems to happen in their lives. I believe strongly that, what makes a New Year is not the change of calendar in your home or office; it goes beyond that. You essentially need to know how to maximize the opportunities set before you in the New Year. You need to discover the life-changing principles that will guide your life in the year; otherwise, the New Year will continue as the old year.

As a matter of necessity, you need to engage in a purposeful sober reflection of your life and make some life-changing decisions that are beyond the realms of the annual rituals of New Year resolutions, which will propel and galvanize you towards the realization of God's purpose for your life.

Studying the Scriptures, from Genesis to Revelation, you will notice that whatever God desires, He speaks and what He speaks immediately manifests. We share similar characteristics as His offspring. The Bible says:

> *"Ye are gods, and all of you are children of the Highest"*. - **Psalm 82:6**

Remember that, greater is He that is in you than he that is in the world and, without any doubt, you are the lord of your words and thoughts. Ask yourself, "What words have I been speaking into my life and into the lives of my children?" Whatever you want, speak it out with faith and God will do it. Are you sick? Speak healing into your life every day. Whatever situation you are passing through, whether positive or negative, speak the Word of God to that situation; become your own prophet. God is willing to reveal all hidden secrets to you if only you will pray and diligently wait to hear from Him. He says:

> *"Call unto me, and I will answer thee, and show thee great and mighty things, which thou knowest not"*
> **Jeremiah 33:3-4**

I beseech you, brethren, to stop migrating, recycling, and shopping for different Churches this year. God is everywhere and He answers every prayer, everywhere. Most people are defeated in their minds without realizing that it all starts with the words in their mouths and the thoughts in their hearts. Think about it: negative evil words ultimately produce pain in your life. The reason is that negative thinking creates negative feelings to produce negative decisions, which leads to negative actions that transform into negative habits and character, which in effect, work against our destiny. Thus, it becomes essential that you decide to be of a positive mind in your attitude toward Christ.

Your achievements and failures, respectively, are the direct results of your words spoken in faith or fear. Our thoughts and words are the access to either the very portal of Heaven or the portal of Hell. When you change the words in your mouth to positive ones, your life will manifest the glory of God.

In Genesis Chapter One, from verse One to the end, we read the story of the creation. God said, let there be light; let there be a firmament amid the waters, and let it divide the waters from the waters; let there be trees, birds, ocean, fishes, animals, fruits, great whales, and every living creature that moved, after its kind, and every winged fowl after its kind and all were done as God said.

"And God saw everything that He had made, and, behold; it was very good; He declared it good."
Genesis 1:31

When God put His faith to work through His spoken Word, to say what He wanted, the heaven and the earth were created. The same applies to you, let the words of your mouth agree with what you desire for yourself and your family by faith in this year and your miracle will manifest. Learn to call the invisible into the visible and declare the impossible to be possible through the words of your mouth.

"A good man out of the good treasure of his heart bringeth forth that which is good; and an evil man out of the evil treasure of his heart bringeth forth that which is evil: for of the abundance of the heart his mouth speaketh."
- Mathew 12:35

"For out of the heart come evil thoughts, murders, adulteries, fornications, thefts, false witness, and slander,"
- Mathew 15:19

The content of your heart will always be the confession of your mouth, which, in turn, determines the characteristics of your life. Be careful therefore what you make the content of your heart.

Chapter 2

Making the Most of Your "God-Given Opportunity"

*I understand how you are already fired up to conquer
mountains and possess the land, to make a difference this year,
but that won't happen until you first reflect, and re-examine
your past.*

Ask yourself what it was that had been stopping you
from fulfilling your destiny for the past years. What
were the challenges that came your way to prevent
you from being fulfilled and maximizing your potential?

Be sincere with yourself, at this juncture: if Jesus were to
appear today or you suddenly discovered that you have
just a few hours to live, just like King Hezekiah, such that
every opportunity God has given you on earth will cease;

money will disappear; cloths, car, house, and all those worldly things that prevented you from moving closer to your Creator and fulfilling your assignment will disappear, and you are left alone with your Maker, will you then boldly stand before Him and tell Him that you maximized and made the most of your divinely given opportunities? If your answer is no, you still have the opportunity now to make things right in your life before it is too late.

Permit me to ask this question and I will appreciate your honest answer: "how many people, since the creation of the earth, do you know or have heard of, who have been able to bribe death away, lobby or make a deal with death and live forever? Definitely, I know your answer will be the obvious, "no one." No one has the potency to live forever. Therefore, hear this, all ye people, declares the Lord, all the inhabitants of the world, both men of low and men of high degree, rich and poor alike:

7 *"No one can pay for the life of anyone else. No one can give God what that would cost.*

8 *The price of a life is very high. No payment is ever enough.*

9 *No one can pay enough to live forever and not rot in the grave.*

¹⁰ Everyone can see that even wise people die People who are foolish and who have no sense also pass away. All of them leave their wealth to others.

¹¹ Their tombs will remain their houses forever. Their graves will be their homes for all time to come. Naming lands after themselves won't help either.

¹² Even though people may be very rich, they don't live on and on. They are like animals. They die.

¹³ That's what happens to those who trust in themselves. It also happens to their followers, who agree with what they say.

¹⁴ They are like sheep and will end up in the grave Death will be their shepherd"
- Psalm 49:7-14

You must come to terms with the fact that death is certain and you cannot do anything about it; secondly, God loved you so much that He gave His only begotten Son to pay the debt of your sin and has given you the free gift of salvation with so many opportunities to make a positive difference in this one lifetime. Don't you think it is high time you made the most of every opportunity given to you by God? Jesus says:

"For what will it profit a man if he gains the whole world and forfeits his soul? Or what will a man give in exchange for his soul?"
- Matthew 16:26

Therefore, brethren, I beseech you in the name of the Lord, to take your first step towards freedom from the system of the world now. Seek the Lord, now, while He may be found.

> [6] *"Seek the LORD while he may be found;*
> *call on him while he is near*

> [7] *Let the wicked forsake their ways and the unrighteous their*
> *thoughts. Let them turn to the LORD, and he will have mercy*
> *on them, and to our God, for he will freely pardon"*
> **- Isaiah 55:6-7**

Understand that, you are not growing any younger and it is appointed unto you to die once and after this judgment (**Hebrew 9:27**).

The clock is ticking by every second and time is going fast! How will you make the most of the opportunity set before you by God before death knocks on your zero hours? Let us explore the Word of God as I will love to share with you how you can make the most of the opportunities God has given you from now on until your zero hours.

Chapter 3

Get Closer to "God"

*There is no doubt about the love of God
for you and that you belong to Him.*

He created you and wants to have a relationship with you; He wants to talk to you and be your best friend.

But you cannot realize how much God loves you until you learn to appreciate what He accomplished on the cross for you; how much He suffered to pay the price of your sin on the cross. This also attests to the fact that you are precious in His sight, and because He loves you, He says, you are His.

Unfortunately, you have been too far away from your God. Now, it is time to come back home to Him and into the relationship, He desires to have with you through Jesus Christ.

You have been living under the guise of religion rather than a relationship with God for too long. You tag it on yourself, saying: I am a Catholic, I am Baptist, I am from Christ Apostolic Church, I am Pentecostal, I am from Second Baptist, I am a Presbyterian, I am from the Redeemed Christian Church of God and the list goes on, but the reality is that, belonging to any denomination is not your ticket to heaven. I am so glad that you will only find true believers, "the saints," in the Presence of God.

"And everyone who calls on the name of the LORD will be saved; for on Mount Zion and in Jerusalem there will be deliverance, as the LORD has said, even among the survivors whom the LORD calls." **- Joel 2:32**

"And everyone who calls on the name of the Lord will be saved." **- Acts 2:21**

"For whosoever shall call upon the name of the Lord shall be saved." **- Romans 10:13** (KJV)

These Scriptures are particular about who shall be saved: it is not being a Pentecostal, an Apostolic, or a member of any denomination that qualifies you as being saved but that you call upon the name of the Lord from a true heart of repentance and recognition that Jesus is the Saviour. Oh Hallelujah! I really praise God that denomination or

Church affiliation is not a ticket to heaven. You essentially need to receive the forgiveness of sin through repentance.

> *"Repent ye therefore, and be converted, that your sins may be blotted out when the times of refreshing shall come from the presence of the Lord."* **- Act 3:19**

If you have never considered it necessary to accept Jesus as your Saviour and Lord and you are not yet born again, you still have the opportunity to do so while you are alive and, in fact, now is the acceptable time; today is the day of salvation. On the other hand, if you are already born again but have backslidden, you will need to rededicate your life to Jesus now.

> *"Salvation is found in no one else, for there is no other name under heaven given to men by which we must be saved"*
> **- Acts 4:12**

This Scripture debunks all other religious claims. Salvation is found in Christ alone. No religion saves and the founders of the religions, themselves, need salvation through Jesus Christ. What Jesus gives you is a relationship with God and not religion. Through fellowship, which is, agreeing with the will of God, we can maintain our relationship with God in Christ. It is pertinent therefore that we resolve to walk in the will of God so we can enjoy unbroken fellowship with God and maintain our relationship with Him, year in, and year out. Affirmatively, the Psalmist says:

> *"My heart says of you "Seek his face!" Your face, LORD, I will seek." -* **Psalm 27:8.**

In the same spirit, Isaiah also says:

> *"My soul yearns for you in the night; in the morning my spirit longs for you. When your judgments come upon the earth, the people of the world learn righteousness" -* **Isaiah 26:9.**

Furthermore, the Psalmist added:

> *"You will show me the path of life; In Your presence is fullness of joy; At Your right hand are pleasures forevermore." -* **Psalm 16:11**

We need God to find true satisfaction and joy in life. It is His Presence that guarantees fullness of joy: the Presence of God gives no room for sorrow or sadness because God is greater than our problems. We should learn therefore to seek more of His Presence than focus on the problem. Life will give us more problems to go through but the Presence of God gives us the fullness of joy, *as Jesus says,*

> *"In the world, ye shall have tribulation: but be of good cheer; I have overcome the world." -* **John 16:33.**

The world we live in was not designed for pain and sadness but sin came in the way and is responsible for the tragedies that now plague human life. Whenever we experience those sad moments in our lives, we need to remember that the only place that can bring refreshment and peace of mind is in a sustained close relationship with God.

Naturally, our faith in God fluctuates. Occasionally, we find ourselves not as close to God as we truly desire. It is usually at those times we feel spiritually weak, depressed, and discouraged by almost everything around us. Situations like this necessitate a conscious effort that can help us recover and maximize the opportunity God is giving us. The Psalmist confirms this to us by his example. He says:

> *"I have set the LORD always before me; because He is at my right hand I shall not be moved."*
> **- Psalms 16:8**

It is when we "**set the Lord before us**" that we receive the benefits of His Presence. Therefore, every time we realize we are beginning to drift away from God, we need to take a retreat from what we are doing to be with the LORD and let Him restore us back to Himself so that the fellowship of His Presence can continue with us.

Chapter 4

Jesus Christ over "Everything"

"Pilate saith unto them, what shall I do then with Jesus, who is called Christ? They all say unto him, let him be crucified"
- Mattew 27:22

Jesus was brought to Pilate to be judged and condemned by Him. In the course of the trial against Him. The question of Pilate still resonates to date and so much depends on finding the right answer to it. It was a very decisive moment for Pilate and his choice would determine his destiny. Likewise, we determine our destiny by the choice we make in life. Proffering the right answer to Pilate's question above can mean having everything in life that is worth having in time and eternity as much as the wrong answer can also mean losing everything worth having now and in eternity. What will become ours if we answer this question right?

Every day, we are faced with the challenge of making the right choice among several options. But most important of all, is our decision for Christ, as implied by Pilate's question. We have the option to either disregard or choose Jesus above other things. We must always remember that we decide our destiny by the choices we make in life.

> [15] *"See, I set before you today life and prosperity, death and destruction.*
>
> [16] *For I command you today to love the LORD your God, to walk in obedience to him, and to keep his commands, decrees, and laws; then you will live and increase, and the LORD your God will bless you in the land you are entering to possess.*
>
> [17] *But if your heart turns away and you are not obedient, and if you are drawn away to bow down to other gods and worship them.*
>
> [18] *I declare to you this day that you will certainly be destroyed. You will not live long in the land you are crossing the Jordan to enter and possess.*
>
> [19] *This day I call the heavens and the earth as witnesses against you that I have set before you life*

and death, blessings and curses. Now choose life, so that you and your children may live.

20. *And that you may love the LORD your God, listen to his voice, and hold fast to him. For the LORD is your life, and he will give you many years in the land he swore to give to your fathers, Abraham, Isaac, and Jacob."*
- **Deuteronomy 30:15-20** (NIV)

The choice you make about what you will do with Jesus is the vehicle that will take you to your future. Moses charged the Israelites to choose between life and death; likewise, you too will have to choose. The Jews rejected Jesus and condemned Him to be crucified. Rather than for Jesus to be freed, they preferred to live under the judgment of God, including their generation to come. Thus, they decided their fate.

Every human being must answer the question, *"what shall I do then with Jesus, who is called Christ?"* as posed by Pilate, to make their choice. Whether you like it or not, you must answer the question. If you are not answering it now, you will definitely answer it when you stand before God in judgment to give an account of your life.

Pilate asked the question, *"what shall I then do with Jesus, who is called Christ?"* two thousand years ago, and yet much still depends on the right answer to the question today. When Pilate asked that question, he was faced with choices, whereby he would determine his destiny.

16

Likewise, we determine our destiny by the choice of what we decide to do with Jesus today. Your choice today will determine your destiny hereafter.

God will not enforce Himself on us but gives us the freedom to choose or make our choices. Whether good or bad, we will always live to bear the consequence or blessings of our choice in life.

Life is about choices. The choices we make also make us. What we are today is the result of the choice we made yesterday and what we shall become tomorrow is dependent on the choice we make today. Therefore, if we fail to make the right choices, our lives will go in the wrong direction and we will miss the future ahead of us. Still, this is not a reason for us to entertain the fear of making a choice. The fear of making a choice is a wrong decision and will only give room to the wrong choice while refusing to make a choice is a choice itself. Therefore, whether you make a choice or fail to make a choice when you need to, there will definitely be an outcome, which will impact on what becomes of you thereafter.

There are consequences for every choice we make; there is either a positive or negative outcome. Wisdom demands therefore that we think about the consequence of a choice before we make it our choice. This will help to ensure you make the right choices all the time.

My father, though not an English speaker, will always say to me in our dialect, *"My son, be careful: the white man (oyinbo) always says, "Think before you act because there will always be a consequence."*

You can choose to sin but you cannot choose the consequence of your sin. Each time we act foolishly because of the wrong choice, we suffer grave consequences that bring pain to us and take our joy away from us. Your life today is the sum total of the results of the choices you have made so far. You can set your life in the right direction by making the right choices. But the right choice depends on being able to discern what is right from what is wrong for you. This is a conscious effort you must make as someone who wants his life to go in the right direction of God for him. If you can control your choice of things, you will be in charge of your life to ensure that you become what God wants you to be in life. This also makes you find the freedom that comes from being in charge of your decision to make the right choices for yourself. But first, you have to choose between surrendering your will to Jesus. This is essential because the effect of your choice, whether good or bad, will continue with you forever.

While growing up, under the care of our parents, we were warned about several things that harm the lives of people, like smoking cigarettes, drinking alcohol, and other harmful substances, to keep us away from them. Despite these warnings, rather than abstain, some people still chose to do these things in their adulthood. They damned the consequences to do these things but eventually, it became the fate they had to live with and suffer for.

Sexual immorality, like fornication and adultery, is another choice we make against ourselves. Despite warnings from God's word, showing that, when we commit such acts, we sin against God and our bodies, some people still choose to make such acts their choice because of the pleasure derived from doing them. But in the long run, the pleasure turns out to be their pain as they became trapped by it because of some sexually transmitted diseases and other related problems.

Unfortunately, when the problem begins with you, the people around you, like family members, share part of it; they worry about you and commit their finances, which would have gone for something much more profitable to them, for your welfare. Nonetheless, the pain is much more on you than those seeing to your welfare; you carry the lion's share of it all. That is to what extent your wrong choice can affect you in life. Your only chance for salvation and survival is to turn to Jesus. He is the consequence that manifests and translates into eternal life with joy and peace. The Bible says:

> 35 *"God has raised this Jesus to life, and we are all witnesses of it...*

> 36 *Therefore let all Israel be assured of this: God has made this Jesus, whom you crucified, both Lord and Messiah.*

> 37 *When the people heard this, they were cut to the heart and said to Peter and the other Apostles, "Brothers, what shall we do?*
>
> 38 *Peter replied, "Repent and be baptized, every one of you, in the name of Jesus Christ for the forgiveness of your sins. And you will receive the gift of the Holy Spirit.*
>
> 39 *The promise is for you and your children and for all who are far off — for all whom the Lord our God will call."*
>
> **- Act 2:36 -39**

God is more interested in your future than in your past. Therefore, leave the past behind you and focus more on the future that is still possible for you. There is nothing you can do about your past than to learn from your mistakes in order to correct your future. It is a most daunting fact that you cannot change your past as well as other things like your history, human nature, parents, birthplace, the laws of physics, and the weather. But one thing is very true: you can change your future and your fate in eternity to come by choosing salvation through Jesus Christ today.

To err is human. No one human is perfect. We cannot be **100%** right with all our choices in life. We have therefore been guilty of wrong choices and mistakes at one time or the other, whatever the case may be, we can still make a difference with the help of God; He makes all things work together for our good. God is a Specialist in turning our mistakes into miracles. He can reverse the situation in your favour. To this end, your wrong choices can change into unbelievable miracles; your test into the testimony; failure into success, and the LORD will move you from the desert to a place of spring freshness and from prison to palace if you turn your heart to Him in genuine repentance and accept His will for your life. Apostle Paul says:

> *"And we know that in all things God works for the good of those who love him, who have been called according to his purpose."*
> **Romans 8:28**

This Scripture is a reality for just some people and not for everybody: it is for "those who love God, who have been called according to his purpose." Therefore, to also be a beneficiary, you have to acknowledge and adhere to the following:

You need to be saved.

The Bible concludes all men are under sin. This also suggests the need for salvation for all men. That's why Jesus came for our redemption. The redemption of Jesus is for the salvation of our souls from sin. But first, you must accept that you are a sinner before you can see the need for the salvation of your soul.

"For all have sinned, and come short of the glory of God" and in"
- Romans 3:23

"There is not a righteous man on earth who does what is right and never sins"
- Ecclesiastes 7:20 (NIV)

"All of us have become like one who is unclean, and all our righteous acts are like filthy rags; we all shrivel up like a leaf, and like the wind, our sins sweep us away."
- Isaiah 64:6

"We all, like sheep, have gone astray, each of us has turned to our own way; and the LORD has laid on him the iniquity of us all."
- Isaiah 53:6

Unless we accept, as the Scriptures declare, that we are sinners, we will not see our need for salvation through Jesus Christ but only tend to claim righteousness by works of religion. There is just one description of the Scripture for our righteousness before God: it is as a filthy rag. Hence, our righteousness is not acceptable before God and cannot make for the salvation of our souls. It is the righteousness of God, which is through faith in Jesus Christ that can save us and make us righteous before God.

Jesus Christ, by His death on the cross, made provision for our salvation and gave us the righteousness of God through His blood that He shed on the cross for our redemption. In Him, therefore, we are given a new life and made righteous before God. That is what it means to be born again. Affirmatively, Jesus says,

> *"Except a man be born again,*
> *he cannot see the kingdom of God."*
> **- John 3:3**.

You cannot save yourself.

The salvation of our souls, which qualifies us for heaven, is not a function of our good works. It doesn't matter how good you are to people and your kind gesture towards men, you still need to be saved. Your good works cannot save you. As good as it is to be good; your good works cannot pay for the salvation of your soul. Charity work and humanitarian projects are good but not an excuse for the salvation of your soul if you will be acceptable before God. It is only the works we do by faith in Christ that count for us in the sight of God. The Bible says:

> *"Not by works of righteousness which we have done, but*
> *according to his mercy he saved us"*
> **- Titus 3:5**

> *"By the works of the law shall no flesh be justified"*
> **- Galatians. 2:16**.

No amount of your good works can make God overlook your sins; they can neither earn you the forgiveness of God. You cannot, therefore, depend on your good work to go to heaven; you must be saved and receive the forgiveness of your sin through faith in Jesus Christ.

It is not your good deeds that commend you to God. To look in the way of your good deeds to be acceptable before God only shows you have been deceived already. To be acceptable before God, you have to look in His way to receive the salvation of your soul and forgiveness of your sin and not look another way.

> *"There is a way which seemeth right unto a man,*
> *but the end thereof are the ways of death"*
> **- Proverbs. 14:12.**

> *"Jesus saith unto him, I am the way, the truth, and*
> *the life: no man cometh unto the Father but by me"*
> **- John 14:6**

To receive the forgiveness of God, you must have first met Christ because He is the only way to the Father, who forgives your sin. Thus also, you learn daily to choose the will of God over every other thing in life.

Jesus has already provided for your salvation.

When Jesus shed His blood to lay down His life for your sin, He paid the price for your salvation and forgiveness of sin to make you righteous before God. The Bible says:

> *"[Jesus] his own self-bare our sins in his own*
> *body on the tree that we, being dead to sins,*

> *should live unto righteousness"*
> **- 1 Peter 2:24**

> *"For Christ also hath once suffered for sins, the just*
> *for the unjust, that he might bring us to God"*
> **- 1 Peter 3:18.**

> *"God made him who had no sin to be sin for us so that*
> *in him we might become the righteousness of God";*
> *you don't need to do anything than to open your earth*
> *and let Jesus in."*
> **- 2 Corinthians. 5:21 NIV**

If you accept all that Jesus suffered to procure the pardon of God for your sin and the salvation of your soul, you will be compelled also to choose to do His will for your life so you can become what He wants you to be in life.

You will have deliverance from the power of Sin.

It is either you are saved or a slave of Satan. Sin makes you a slave to Satan. By sin, Satan enslaved man in the beginning. Everyone therefore who is yet to be saved from sin is a slave of the devil. It is only in Jesus Christ that we have salvation, which gives us deliverance. The Bible says:

> *"If the Son sets you free, you will be free indeed"*
> **- John 8:36 NIV.**

> *"He came to that which was his own, but his own did*
> *not receive him. Yet to all who received him, to those*
> *who believed in his name, he gave the right to become*

children of God, children born not of natural descent,
nor of human decision or a husband's will, but born of
*God" - **John 1:11–13 NIV***

It is Jesus Christ, who gives the power to become "children of God." It implies therefore that those who are yet to meet Christ and accept Him as their Saviour and Lord are not enlisted among the children of God. Hence, I beseech you in the name of the Lord,

"Believe in the Lord Jesus, and you will be saved"
- Acts 16:31, NIV

Turn from sin in genuine repentance.

Repentance is our first response to the truth of the gospel that saved our souls because, by it, we are willing to turn away from our sin to fulfill the will of God for our lives. We cannot receive the offer of salvation and the forgiveness of sin, which are available to us in Christ Jesus, without repentance.

"Now [God] commands all people everywhere to repent"
- Acts 17:30, NIV.

*"Repent, then, and turn to God, so that your sins may be wiped out" - **Acts 3:19, NIV.***

*"Repent and believe the good news!" - **Mark 1:15** NIV*

God demands total and complete repentance from you. There is no acceptance to the household of faith without genuine repentance from sin. Jesus loves you and accepts you just as you are when you come to Him in repentance but He requires that you turn away from your old ways or sinful habits.

Repentance denotes a change of heart, which also results in a change of attitude from sinfulness to righteousness. The heart of repentance, therefore, makes you always choose the will and ways of God for your life in all things; thus, you can also live to fulfill the purpose of God for you and become all that God wants you to be in life.

Chapter 5

Shun "Ignorance!"

"God's people are destroyed for lack of knowledge."
- Hosea 4:6

Ignorance is lethal in effect; it makes a man unable to see the consequences of his actions and be responsible for his own self-destruction as a result. A man of ignorance is uninformed and lacks direction for his life. This also makes life a struggle for him and succeeding is usually a herculean task for him. Ignorance of God's Word does something similar to us when it comes to fulfilling God's purpose for us. Our fulfillment in life is a result of the Word practice, whereby we align with God's will for our lives. The Bible says:

*"This Book of the Law shall not depart from your
mouth, but you shall meditate in it day and night, that
you may observe to do according to all that is written
in it. For then you will make your way prosperous, and
then you will have good success"*
- Joshua 1:8

Nothing can take the place of God's Word in our walk with Him. You may be prayerful; but still, you need to be established in the will of God. The Word of God gives us the instructions of God, which helps to establish us in the will of God so our walk with God can be effective to help us achieve His purpose for us in life. Apostle Peter says:

*"His divine power has given us everything we need for
a godly life through our knowledge of him who called
us by his own glory and goodness."*
- 2 Peter 1:3

It is impracticable to live a godly life and enjoy the accompanying power and blessings of God with it without the knowledge of God, Himself. It is through the knowledge of God that His divine power has given us everything we need for a godly life. The knowledge of God is only found in His Word. The Word of God gives us the revelation of God; it makes God known to us. Therefore, our lives can only align with His will when we live by His Word. But that is only possible when we are enlightened with the knowledge of Him by His Word. The Word of God only becomes meaningful to us by the knowledge of

God that it gives to us when we study it while the knowledge of God, in turn, gives us everything that we need to be godly, and being godly comes with the power and blessings of God. To this end, we are required to take delight in God's Word.

> 1 *"Blessed is the man, Who walks not in the counsel of the ungodly, Nor stands in the path of sinners, Nor sits in the seat of the scornful;*
>
> 2 *But his delight is in the law of the LORD, And in His law, he meditates day and night.*
>
> 3 *He shall be like a tree Planted by the rivers of water, That brings forth its fruit in its season, Whose leaf also shall not wither; And whatever he does shall prosper."*
> **- Psalm 1:1-3**

This Scripture gives us the description of the blessed man; he is the man who delights in the Word of God and that makes him different from the other man who looks elsewhere for counsel and is given to the pleasures of life. Nothing else makes a man's life meaningful and fruitful like God's Word does for us. Ignorance of God's Word, therefore, makes your life like the labour of the foolish because you cannot know the leading of God for you therewith.

> *The labour of fools wearies them, for they do not even know how to go to the city!*
> **- Ecclesiastes 10:15**

There is a destination for every one of us in life. Your destination in life also means your destined end. Unless you are in the right direction for your life, you cannot get to your destination in life. It is God's Word alone that can give you the right direction for your life. It establishes you in the will of God for you so that you can become all that God wants you to be in life. That is the definition of success as far as God is concerned.

Success, by God's standard, is measured by what you were created to do, be or become in line with God's will and purpose for your life. Hence, you cannot achieve the success that God desires for you outside of His will for your life. Thus, it becomes essential to know God's will for you and make His purpose for your life your pursuit in life. Be careful not to compare yourself with others and never try to do or be like them; you were not created to be the carbon copy of someone else.

The devil wants you to miss the assignment or purpose of God for your life; therefore, he comes to you with different distractions in life. He doesn't want you to achieve the success of God for you but the success of the world. The Bible, therefore, warns us to be mindful of his devices so he will not take advantage of us. Apostle Paul says:

> *"Lest Satan should get an advantage of us:*
> *for we are not ignorant of his devices"*
> **- 2 Corinthians 2:11**

Your ignorance of God's will for you is the devil's advantage over you. As long as you are living in ignorance of God's will for you, the devil will continue to prevail over you with his deceptive schemes. The Bible is the only antidote for this; it gives you the knowledge of God's Word so you can know and live in the will of God for you.

Beware! The devil's tricks are not hidden or new. They are the same tricks, as ever before, that he is still using now, though introduced in another format or pattern to deceive us. We can find out these tricks with the help of the Holy Spirit when we read the Bible. The activities of the devil are all aimed at achieving his mission over mankind. Jesus gives this revelation to us. He says:

> *"The thief cometh not, but for to steal, and to kill, and to destroy: I am come that they might have life and that they might have it more abundantly"*
> **- John 10:10**

Jesus is anti to the devil; He came to undo all the works of the devil against us, so we can fulfill the purpose of God for us in the world. Jesus, therefore, provides the salvation of our souls to us but it is our responsibility to defend this salvation by the full realization of its significance to us. This endears us further into spiritual warfare against the devil and all the powers working for him. The Bible says:

> *"For we wrestle not against flesh and blood, but against principalities, against powers, against the rulers of the darkness of this world, against spiritual*

wickedness in high places"
- Ephesians 6:12

First of all, this Scripture gives us the awareness that we are in warfare; it further gives us the revelation of who we are in the warfare with: they are persons without bodies or spiritual foes. Thus, it is called spiritual warfare. These enemies are always there contending with our destiny, whether we fight or not. Hence, it becomes essential for us to fight and not pretend or claim ignorance about the fight. If you are going to fulfill your destiny in the world, you must rise up in spiritual warfare and fight against the enemies of your soul.

Ignorance is not an excuse in spiritual warfare. It is the reason for the misfortunes of so many Christians and why they cannot fulfill their destiny. It takes the wisdom of God to adopt the right strategy for winning spiritual warfare. With wisdom, you can always know the right weapon to use in different situations and in the right way. That's why wisdom is very essential. The Bible says:

"Wisdom is the principal thing; therefore get wisdom, and with all thy getting, get understanding"
- Proverbs 4:7

Wisdom is profitable to direct.
- Ecclesiastes 10:10

Wisdom is the application of facts. It is the practical side of knowledge because it helps you know what you are to do with what you know so you can succeed with it. Thus, wisdom is essential in all spheres of life. The lack of it only makes you foolish. That's why only fools despise wisdom (Proverbs 1:7b).

Chapter 6

Take Charge of "Your Day"

"In the morning, LORD, you hear my voice; in the morning I lay my requests before you and wait expectantly."
Psalm 5:3

"My soul yearns for you in the night; in the morning my spirit longs for you. When your judgments come upon the earth, the people of the world learn righteousness."
Isaiah 26:9.

*E*very day with the peace of God is very essential. It helps you to be in charge of the day and take advantage of every opportunity that the day offers to you. But you can only avail yourself of the peace of God by taking charge of the day at the beginning of the day in God's presence. It means to start the day with God in His Presence. Before you set out into the day to start doing anything and meeting people, talk to God first and commit the day unto Him, otherwise, the day may not go as expected. Don't place priority on your daily schedule and engagements over God because God is the Owner of each day and you need the peace that His Presence brings to make a difference in each day. Therefore, make it a habit to always start your day with God; talk to Him, first thing in the morning and commit the day unto Him, before you start the day. This is your guarantee for a peaceful and prosperous day.

Don't be casual in your practice of starting the day with God; be intentional. Spend quality time in the Presence of God, talking to Him about the day. Shun the habit of rushing to pray because you want to rush into the day for your engagements. It should not be when you are already at the door of your house to go out that you remember to pray and all you do is, hold the door half open, with one step inside and one step outside, and manage to pray as a last minute thing; this is as good as not praying at all.

Communication with God is a great privilege that our relationship with God avails us. We don't need any intermediary to communicate with God other than our relationship with Him through Jesus Christ. We must therefore learn to take advantage of our relationship with God to communicate with Him. Communication is the greatest asset in love and the best of God is reserved for those who love Him.

"However, as it is written: "What no eye has seen, what no ear has heard, and what no human mind has conceived" the things God has prepared for those who love him"
1 Corinthians 2:9

God has some things in store, which He has prepared for our fulfillment in life. But these things are only accomplished for those who love God; they are not for everybody. Unless we comprehend the love of God and reciprocate it to Him, we cannot take advantage of these things to live a fulfilled life as God desires and designs for us. Rather, we will only complain daily about life and despair over praying without getting an answer to our requests.

The love of God in our hearts compels us daily to long for His Presence and desist from things that offend Him. Thus, we get used to His Presence and secure His Presence with us always. Through this, we find favour before Him as He also brings us into favour with men for the things He has prepared for those who love Him so that we may live a fulfilled life. You cannot have the reality of God's presence with you and suffer what is called ill luck or bad luck in life. The Presence of God will always make a difference.

When you are not always in contact with God but keep a distance from His Presence, He becomes silent in your life.

You only get to realize this in your time of distress when you need to hear from God to know what to do but He doesn't seem to be speaking. Unfortunately, instead of realizing their distance from God and returning to Him, most Christians rather begin to chase after every revival and miracle programme and run after "men of God" but only to fall into the hands of those who will only make merchandise of them in their search for a microwave answer from God. Furthermore, they tend to yield to any suggestion from men about their situation but only to complicate matters for themselves. Oh! What peace we often forfeit; oh! What needless pain we bear; all because we do not carry everything to God in prayer. Seeking God early in the morning is the secret to the believer's triumph in life.

If you desire to have a joyful, happy, and successful day, take charge of your day early in the morning. As we seek God early we will never lack but will be lightened, empowered, and all shame will end in our lives (Psalm 34:5); durable riches and honor will be given to us, also (Proverbs 8:17). When you seek Him, He will give you rest

> *"Come unto me, all ye that labour and are heavily laden, and I will give you rest"*
> - **Matthew 11:28**.

Abundant rest means grace for faith in God to do exploits so that you may be triumphant in life.

I remember early in February 2010, during our workers and ministers meeting, Evangelist Bola Dunmoye and Evangelist Elizabeth Lawal suggested that we start an online Prayer. We deliberated on the issue and concluded that we should pray and meditate on it. We did not want to start a Prayer Line just because many Churches were doing the same; we decided that we would start it only if the Lord instructed us to do so. We chose to seek the face of God for His direction. A few months later, we had the green light to proceed and we started. A year later, during one of our three days of prayer and fasting in the Church, the Lord led us to start a Yoruba Prayer Line called **"AJIGBARE"** as an arm of '**BasiriBasiri**' Prayer Ministry in Nigeria. Amazingly, this prayer program positively affected my prayer life as much as I believe it helped the members too. The Prayer program helped me to know the value of early Morning Prayer and the act of taking charge of the day. If you want to maximize your divine opportunity this year, you must know how to take charge of your day early in the morning.

Most people dread these three words – *'Early'*, *'Morning'*, and *'Prayer'*. When you put all three of those words together, it only makes some people faint. I'm not sure I know of anyone who loves to wake up from a deep slumber, let alone wake up before sunrise just to pray. Everybody must have said this statement, at least once in their lifetime: "I'm not a morning person."

As much as I have heard people often declare that they are not morning people, I am yet to hear people say or declare that *"I'm not an afternoon person"* or *"I'm not an evening person."* Those times (*afternoon and night*) are always good for them. However, when you ask them how important early Morning Prayer is or throw the word, "prayer" around them, you will get funny responses, especially from those who feel guilty about their lack of consistent early Morning Prayer. The question is: if people know how important Morning Prayer is, as a daily activity, why are they not doing it fervently?

I remember when I was about 8 or 10 years old, growing up at Ilu-Abo Village, about one hour drive to Akure (Metro-City), my hometown in Nigeria, I was living with my grandmother then, who happened to be a prayer warrior. My grandfather was a church planter and our house happened to be next to the mission house. Every day, from Monday to Friday, at 4.30 am, you will hear the big prayer time bell ring very loudly, waking up everyone. By 5.00 am everybody would gather in front of the mission house ready for the early morning prayers.

My main assignment was to carry the gas lamp ahead of the entire village, singing, dancing, and praising the Lord as we would always walk more than 6 miles round trip every morning and evening to both the morning and evening worship services. I did this for several years, so much that I would not allow anyone to carry the Gas Lamp and I would lead the village to church early in the morning and also lead them back on the return from the evening service. It was to the extent that I was nicknamed the "**Lamp Carrier**" which to me was a great honor.

My grandmother and my mother laid prayer foundations for my life and when my grandmother passed unto glory, I relocated to Akure, where I joined the choir of another church. I later became a member of a group called 'CAC, Light of the World Society' led by Pastor Bayo Ijelu. This group transformed my life and my association with Christ Apostolic Church, Light of the World Society became a life-changing experience when it came to 'Prayer' and the 'Word'. The climax of my spiritual growth came when God started the 'BasiriBasiri' Prayer Mountain. Oh my God! It was such an awesome experience that cannot be fully explained. When you experience the transforming power of God, you will not be able to explain in detail how you feel; it's beyond words and illustrations.

The Morning Prayer can be a tremendous source of power in the life of the Christian who has resolved to meet God daily. If you make it a lifestyle, you are certain to also find that every assurance and promise given in Scripture is true. Seeking God early in the morning is the secret to the believer's triumph in life.

We are not sufficient in ourselves to pray; we do not know how to pray, nor do we know what to pray about. The spirit of man is weak and cannot penetrate deep into the things of the spirit, but glory be to God in the highest who has given us the Holy Spirit to enable us with divine strength to do what we cannot do in prayer and also to teach us all things.

> [5] *"Not that we are competent in ourselves to claim anything for ourselves, but our competence comes from God.*
>
> [6] *He has made us competent as ministers of a new covenant - not of the letter but of the Spirit; for the letter kills, but the Spirit gives life."*
> **- 2 Corinthians 3:5-6**

> [26] *"In the same way, the Spirit helps us in our weakness. We do not know what we ought to pray for, but the Spirit himself intercedes for us through wordless groans.*
>
> [27] *And he who searches our hearts knows the mind of the Spirit because the Spirit intercedes for God's people in accordance with the will of God."*
> **- Romans 8:26-27**

> *"for it is God who works in you to will and to act in order to fulfill his good purpose."*
> **- Philippians 2:13**

Our sufficiency is of God and as we seek Him early, we will never lack because we will be enlightened and all the efforts of the enemy over our lives will be null and void.

"Those who look to him are radiant; their faces are never covered with shame, durable riches, and honor will be given to us"
- Psalm 34:5

I can honestly tell you that it is not easy to get up before sunrise and spend quality time in prayer and even Bible reading. Worst still, it is not easy, at all, when you force yourself to go to bed earlier every day. The fact is that nobody was given the gift of waking early or sleeping early from heaven; it is just a matter of discipline and determination.

Getting up early to pray will never be an easy walk in the park, but if you can do it, the blessing and joy therein are immeasurable. You need to maximize your divine opportunity this year; take charge of your day with prayer, and read the Word of God early in the morning before you do anything. The benefits are tremendous to your spiritual life when consistently done. There's just nothing quite like getting up early and praying before anything else is done. Here is the mystery: when you are up praying early, you will find that your mind doesn't wander and there will be no crazy thoughts to distract you, compared to when you pray during the day.

Secondly, the spirit world is usually at rest during the early morning time so you will have to wake up and pray. During the day, the devil works through the human body or flesh and all his demonic spirits gather all night to plan to kill, destroy and pull down. So, waking up before sunlight, what you realize is that many people are still sleeping, and even the mediums through which the enemies work are also at rest because they stop their mischievous deeds at about 3:00 am. Taking advantage of this, in your Morning Prayer, you should begin to prophesy, bind and loose, take charge and control, tear down, uphold, and finally command the day, the sun, the moon, every creation, and man to work in your favour and not to work against you. This gives you the privilege of demolishing all the plans your spiritual enemy had made on your life during the midnight hours which they intend to carry out against you during the day.

You will feel much more accomplished when you get up early to pray and take control of the rest of the day. Consequent upon this, you also feel less frazzled trying to find time during the day to pray since you already accomplished your spiritual task in the early hours of the day.

Early Morning Prayers are the key to a happy, successful, and godly day. Besides praying to be led by the Holy Spirit in your early Morning Prayer, there are hundreds of things to pray about before you step out to begin the day's activities.

They include:

Always make sure you attract or are fully connected to the Presence of God. Don't go any further until you feel that God is looking down at you with the eyes of love and that He is listening to your prayer. You will be fully assured that His Holy Spirit is working with you.

Secondly, renew your covenant with God, promising to walk with Him daily; resolve, every morning, to obey Christ absolutely, and tell God that you want to walk faithfully in all His teachings during the day. In your prayer, ask and receive in faith the very grace and power you are specifically in need of. As you start each day, firmly resolve that your guiding principle throughout the day will be to walk faithfully with God.

Thirdly, confess your sins openly to God. Let your confession of sin be very truthful and sincere from a humble heart. Resolve to pluck out and cut off everything that has been grieving God in your life. Pray specifically for grace in certain areas where you are weak; remember you are to walk holy before Him at all times.

Fourthly, you will need to intercede for others; both in your family and for those that are not; stand in the gap for them on a daily basis.

And finally renew your mind by reading the Word of God, with the aim of receiving a direct word from Him. While reading the word, you will be lifted and fed spiritually.

> *"And the LORD turned the captivity of Job when he prayed for his friends: also the LORD gave Job twice as*

> *much as he had before."*
> **- Job 42:7-10**

Praying for friends is what improved Job's life. Moses' sister, Miriam, rebelled against Moses' leadership instead of encouraging him. She was struck with leprosy and immediately Moses cried out and interceded for her.

> *"O God, I beg you, please heal her. God answered Moses' prayer and healed her."* **- Number 12:13**

I wondered if Moses remembered how Job's life turned around for the better after he prayed for his friends at the time when he prayed for his sister. Either way, the outcome was the same. There are wonderful blessings in store for those who pray for others, especially when we pray for those who have not been a comfort but a pain to us. Intercede on behalf of others.

In His relationship with the Father, Jesus did all things for the benefit of others. This same spirit should flow through every member of Christ's body here on earth. The more we recognize this and mold our lives accordingly, the more our lives will be in harmony with what God wishes for us to be. The highest type of prayer is intercession.

Beware that, if you only use prayer as a means of personal improvement and joy, you won't realize its full power. Nonetheless, when you intercede for others, let it be a real genuine longing for the souls prayed for. If you want to maximize your divine opportunity, then, learn how to pray for others, for you are of a royal priesthood.

Let me share with you how you can start taking charge of your day:

First and foremost, go to bed earlier. Staying up till late at night when you know you will have to wake up early is not going to work in the accomplishment of this mission, irrespective of what you may believe. Try to cut back on watching TV before you go to bed; it is hard to turn it off once you've been watching it for hours on end. Try reading a book to get you to fall asleep early in the night.

Secondly, set more than one alarm clock. A good trick of mine is to set an alarm that will jar me awake 30 minutes earlier and then set a couple more around the time I want to get up. I like to get up around 5 am, so I set an alarm around 4:30 am and then set a few more before 5 am. I will also set an alarm across the room, not close to my bed, so I would have to leave the comfort of my bed and covers to go turn it off, forcing me to wake up.

Thirdly, set a prayer time length goal. Set a goal for how long you would like to pray. Start small, and then build up from there. It is good to set attainable goals. Keep track of the time you got up and the time you finished praying. This will keep you motivated to keep progressing towards a mark.

Finally, try the early Morning Prayer for at least a month and see how it will work for you. After all, if you buy any product from the store, they will tell you, if you are not satisfied with it, you have a 30 days return policy and a money-back guarantee.

Maximize your opportunity this year; trying early Morning Prayer for one day won't give you a feel of what you are trying to accomplish. Try it for a month and check your progress. If you do not see any positive result in your life, health, and family, you will get a 30-day prayer return policy from the Holy Spirit; go back to Him and ask Him for answers as to why nothing happened during your dedicated time of prayer. I guarantee you, He will never hide anything from you but tell you the truth and nothing but the truth. He will tell you why your prayer is not answered or why it is being delayed.

Early Morning Prayer isn't for everyone. Some enjoy late-night prayer. My stand and word of encouragement to you are that you are consistently praying at your preferred time of the day. However, if you want to shake things up a bit in your prayer life, you need a place to get started, I suggest giving early Morning Prayer a try. The **"AJIGBARE"** (Waking up early to receive God's blessings) Yoruba Prayer Line is a simple way to start. Find out more on our Facebook.

Chapter 7

Jettison "Complacency" and "Procrastination"

Complacency and procrastination are plaques that destroy destinies as much as they also waste valuable time and divine resources.

Complacency is the mother of mediocrity while procrastination is the father of poverty and failure.

Brethren! Procrastination is a plaque in the Christian community.

In my 35 years of ministry, I have witnessed in the life of thousands of Christian brothers and sisters, across every gender and race, an epidemic called "**complacency and procrastination**". We, Christians, can pray! We know how to fast; how to stay on the mountain, pray, and fast for 21 days. We know how to talk well; how to put together a good plan that may lead us to a breakthrough. We know how to prophesy; how to pull the devil down and crush Satan's head. We know how to stand in the gap for someone else; how to lift our eyes unto the hill expecting miracles to come. We are experts in calling things that are not into being by faith. But in the area of action and doing things at the appointed time and season, we are deficient. We procrastinate and complain so much that the angels are fed up with so many people; they won't come near to minister to such because their procrastination is an act of disobedience and lack of faith in Jesus.

Some time ago, I had the pleasure of being acquainted with a dear brother and his wife, who later became members of our church. Believe me, they loved the Lord and they were very humble, dedicated, fervent, and well-seasoned with the word. After some time, they began to experience a financial downturn in their lives; the brother's car was repossessed, and his house was about to be foreclosed; his wife cried out to me, saying, 'Pastor you need to talk to my husband'. I immediately did quick research in the church accounting and record and discovered that he wasn't faithful in his tithe and offering. Then, I called him so we could talk.

During our conversation, I was shocked when he said, "Pastor, I don't think God answers prayer in this church." I said, *"why not, what happened?"* He said, "Since I joined this church, I have seen others giving dumbfounding testimonies, but I have never received any miracle, especially for those things that I have been asking God for". I then questioned him, "what was your prayer request?" He said, "I had been praying and trusting God that He would speak to someone, somewhere, anywhere; give him my name and address, and instruct the individual to give me a check of one million dollars, or someone would knock on my door and pay all my unpaid bills or I would just open my mail and find a check of one million dollars to prove that God answers prayers". I laughed and said, "Listen, I will like to ask you a question". "How many souls have you won for Christ this year?" "None," he said. How faithful have you been in paying your tithe? At this, he had no answer. I continued. "First, do you not know that when you do not pay your Tithe faithfully, you put yourself under a curse? No miracle will come your way."

Secondly, "Almost two years ago, we sat down together like this"; we discussed and prayed about the vision God had placed in your heart, which for ten good years you did nothing about it and yet you promised me at that time that you would start the Traveling Agency business since you have been in the Travel industry for more than 20 years.

This is the 2nd year since we had that talk. You still have not done anything about it. Your famous excuse has always been, 'I will start it next week or I will start it next month' and I remember asking you the question: "do you not know that when God gives someone a divine assignment or opportunity, it has a time frame attached to it; when you fail to recognize it, or maybe you recognized it, but due to complacency and procrastination you never make use of the opportunity, Heaven will withdraw that assignment from you and give it to the next person in line?"

At this junction, he started crying. I encouraged him with the Word of God and I told him it is not over until God says it is over. God is merciful and gracious; He can still give you another opportunity if you will be serious with it."

Many of us are like this Christian Brother; you would have experienced more blessings if not for the fact that you procrastinate, complain, and waste so much valuable time doing nothing. Brethren, as a Pastor, I am tired of hearing Christian brothers and sisters saying, "Pastor, I will start going to school next semester; Pastor, don't worry, I will do it tomorrow." In fact, calling 'Pastor' has become such a good melodious song or music in their mouth, that it has now become tiresome.

Many Christians have lost their calling and the great opportunities that God has given them because they only know how to talk the talk but cannot walk the talk.

In Maryland, 1999, we had a Guest Minister from South Africa in our Church, Christ Apostolic Church, Vineyard of Comfort, Lanham, Maryland. During his preaching, he said, the Lord gave him a message, titled: "*The prayer of Jabez*". That was 1997, about two years ago. Then, he said, he had preached the message in his Church and because of his obedience to follow instructions, God opened more doors for him to minister in over 20 different Churches. He went on to say that, several people, including his fellow Pastors, told him to turn the message into a book and title it "*The Prayer of Jabez*", but due to procrastination and complacency, he never did. A few years later, God inspired another man of God, ("*the next person in line for the divine assignment*") to write a book and he called it "*The Prayer of Jabez*", and was published here in the United States around the same period this man spoke about. The author has sold over 10 million copies of this book.

> *When we complain and procrastinate we lose our divine harvest and blessing.*

The fact is that complacent Christians make no serious attempt to improve on their daily work and yet they wonder why their business success, customers, and many good things are passing them by regularly. If, as a Christian, you are going to succeed in life, you must not be complacent. A complacent person feels so satisfied with the success of yesterday that he is unable to see more successes ahead.

> *"Woe to the complacent in Zion..."*
> **Amos 6:1** (*The New American Bible*)

I know you desperately want a divine change to happen in your life. I know you desire a breakthrough and some financial freedom. I know that you know that your season of favour has come. However, you need to face the reality of your life. You cannot continue to complain and procrastinate and expect miracles. You have to do whatever it takes to stop wasting your golden time. Look at your life now; how old are you now? Guess what, you can never gain back those years that are gone again; they are gone, forever.

The only option and opportunity you have now are to return and settle with your Maker, repent, and receive your dream back again. It is not too late right now, but it will be too late soon. You can still start the project; even though you are hard-pressed on every side, you will not be crushed or perplexed. Though your fig tree is not blossoming and there is no fruit in your vine now, God has not forsaken you. This message is for you:

> *"Fear thou not; for I am with thee: be not dismayed; for*
> *I am thy God: I will strengthen thee; yea, I will help*
> *thee; yea, I will uphold thee with the right hand of my*
> *righteousness. I the Lord will make a way for you."*

You are coming back again with glory, honor, and success in Jesus' name. Amen. Hallelujah!

Chapter 8

Learn from the Past and "Let it Go"

The secret of success is hidden in how we apply what we learn from past experiences to our new and current situations.

You must learn from past experiences but leave the past behind you; your best years are still ahead.

Perhaps, you made some mistakes and failed to achieve some of your goals or even got disappointed by some people. The fact remains that such experiences will always abound, especially when we put our trust in the arm of flesh and not God. But whenever they happen, we should learn our lesson from them and forge ahead, rather than crying over them till they become a reason for us to start feeling discouraged.

You cannot continue to mourn over your Saul but arise with your horn of oil and let God lead you to find and anoint your David. When we reflect on the future, we are not to allow the events of the past to becloud our vision. While Samuel was reflecting on the future of Israel, he allowed the past mistake of Saul to becloud his vision until God intervened to make him see a new hope for Israel.

> *"Now the Lord said to Samuel, 'You have mourned long enough for Saul. I have rejected him as king of Israel, so fill your flask with olive oil and go to Bethlehem. Find a man named Jesse who lives there, for I have selected one of his sons to be my king."*
> **1 Samuel 16:1** (NLT)

You have mourned long enough, says the Lord. You have cried long enough about the runaway man; you have wailed too much over your disappointment; you have dwelt much too long on the story of the person who offended you 30 years ago when you were 10 years old. Now, at age 45, you are still holding on to it; grieving over it; having sleepless nights and you can't move forward. Even to the extent of giving excuses, like: if not because of the divorce, your life would have been better; if not because of the death of your father, your mother, or someone you once loved and the list goes on, you would have done this and that. Get up! Says the Lord! King Saul has lost his crown; he has been rejected. Fill your flask with olive oil (You will be filled with the Holy Spirit!) and move on with your life and go on to look for your David; look for another opportunity. Stop sitting at the beautiful gate; enter your temple, jump up, run, dance, and praise the Lord.

What you do not know is that, as long as you sit at the gate complaining and feeling sorry for yourself, you are having a pity party, and you will never experience what it means to be free from bondage. Don't forget the Church is waiting to rejoice with you. There is a glory that is about to be revealed in your life, the world is anxious and patiently waiting for you to get up and stop complaining. Concerning the impotent man, the Bible says:

> 6 *"When Jesus saw him lying there and learned that he had been in this condition for a long time, he asked him, "Do you want to get well?*
>
> 7 *"Sir," the invalid replied, "I have no one to help me into the pool when the water is stirred. While I am trying to get in, someone else goes down ahead of me.*
>
> 8 *Then Jesus said to him, "Get up! Pick up your mat and walk.*
>
> 9 *At once the man was cured; he picked up his mat and walked."*
> **- John 5:6-9**

This man is the carbon copy of many Christians. For 38 long years, he was paralyzed and someone always took advantage of him, just like you; whenever he tried to get into the water, he was never given the opportunity, just like you, also. For some, it is that 'the pastor offended me.' Some will even dare to say, God offended them and they want revenge. What a terrible life to live!

The paralytic man was daily sitting by the pool; he probably begged for his living, and people gave him money and food. His friends had abandoned him, and no one cared for him or looked after his welfare; thus, he was desolate and helpless. However, the poolside became a comfort zone and easy shelter for him because he found solace from the food and money received as alms from sympathizers at the poolside and he eagerly looked forward to them helping his condition. But if healed, he would forfeit all of these benefits and start working; nevertheless, his healing was still important to him. As much as he depended on the alms received at the pool, he still needed to get healed so he can start working and living a better life.

Does the story seem familiar to you? Do you not despair to work because of food stamps or being content with your current salary? Yet, you complain that you are poor? For 38 years, the paralytic man accepted this condition. Though he was not happy with his condition, yet he accepted it as a fate that cannot be changed. Whenever the angel troubled the water, he always had excuses, as someone would step on his toe, someone offended him, someone won't take him into the water, someone said some bad words to him, someone looked down on him, someone did not appreciate him, and the list goes on and on.

We must jettison excuses if we are going to cooperate with the will of God for us to achieve the success He destined for us. I discovered something very annoying in the Christian fold: whenever there is a misunderstanding between brothers or sisters in the Church, the next thing is that they will stop coming to the regular Church program; before you know it, they have changed Church and when asked why, they'll always reply, "the Lord is leading us to move on". Some, who are Ministers, will even lie in the name of the Lord, saying, "The Lord is leading us to start our own ministry" when in reality, they were simply angry about something that happened. The truth is that they just want to be independent. But they could have chosen to be honest about it and do things appropriately and godly. This has prompted me many times that I felt like asking them why they thought it necessary to tell lies against God, rather than being honest and putting the devil to shame. Unfortunately, they have made their decisions based on grudges, hatred, and anger. They only found themselves in such strange situations just because they refused to let go of old hurtful experiences at the juncture of their success.

Regrettably, the evil of their wrong decision will continue to hunt them as they go on. The enemy will always rise up against them, using someone to scratch their old wounds. Then, they suffer the same fate (of what they did where they left) as a result. You wonder why so many ministers fail in the course of their ministry! It's because their foundation is faulty.

Can you believe that, because of what someone did or did not do, this man wasted 38 good years of his life just like that! Maybe you are in a similar situation, and someone has done things to you 30 years, 15 years, or even a long time ago; you need to let it go and stop using it as an excuse. The Spirit of the Lord says, though it is very painful and you are hurt and disappointed; you can still go back to reconcile and rebuild your faulty foundation and then move on from there. Your Sarah has died, and that is painful, however, you must bury your death and move on in strength.

> 2 *"And Sarah died in Kirjatharba; the same is Hebron in the land of Canaan: and Abraham came to mourn for Sarah, and to weep for her.*
>
> 3 *And Abraham stood up from before his dead, and spake unto the sons of Heth, saying,*
>
> 4 *I am a stranger and a sojourner with you: give me a possession of a burying place with you, that I may bury my dead out of my sight."*
> **- Genesis 23: 2-4**

You must bury your death out of your sight too; you just have to let it go if you want to make heaven. One of the main reasons you must let go is that the individual that hurt you has moved on. He or she is not even thinking about you anymore but is having fun with life, yet here you are still angry and upset. I pray the Lord will help you to understand my point. Put an end to your mourning!

> *"Then again Abraham took a wife,*
> *and her name was Keturah"*
> **- Genesis 25:1**

After the failure, the cry, and the disappointment, you must make another move. After your last failed exam, you must rewrite another one; prepare for the next interview after that last rejection; expect another pregnancy after you lost that beautiful baby. Don't stop until you receive your joy.

> *"Adam had sexual relations with his wife again, and*
> *she gave birth to another son. She named him Seth, for*
> *she said, 'God has granted me another son in place of*
> *Abel, whom Cain killed."*
> **- Genesis 4:25** (NLT)

May I let you know that, if you take a step of faith now; God will give you your Seth to replace the Abel that you lost in the name of Jesus? You have indeed prayed for many years for that miracle without result, you still need to pray again and believe God one more time for the miracle; God will give you your Samuel that is waiting to be born.

"...and the Lord remembered her [Hannah]"
- 1 Samuel 1:19 (KJV)

She became pregnant and gave birth to Samuel. The same God that remembered Hannah will remember you. The Lord will bless you with your Samuel in Jesus' name.

What are the challenges that you are facing today? You may have been praying for a solution for years without any answer or change and now the problem no longer looks abnormal because it seems to have become part of your daily lifestyle as a condition that has been there for way too long.

You may have a life where there is no peace; it could be that the same sickness haunts you every day. Behold, your season has come for divine intervention and change. You just need to forget your negative and painful past and believe in God for the best season now.

After 38 years, the man at the pool got up and walked again; you too will rise again and your destiny shall not be limited. Abraham buried his death out of his sight; you too will never see your problem again in Jesus' name.

Your moment has come to place your unwavering trust in the omniscience of God. He truly cares about you and He loves you profoundly. Believe in the promises of Jesus and approach this New Year hoping for a great one in the presence of the living Christ. He will guide you through the labyrinth of life because He knows what is best for you.

Your duty lies in obeying Him. Your anxiety, your pain, and your terrible and unpleasant past will be replaced with a glorious future masked with joy unspeakable.

> *"No, dear brothers and sisters, I have not achieved it, but I focus on this one thing: Forgetting the past and looking forward to what lies ahead, I press on to reach the end of the race and receive the heavenly prize for which God, through Christ Jesus, is calling us"*
> **- Philippians 3:13-14** (NLT)

No matter what happened last year, believe that this New Year provides many more new windows of opportunities for a better experience under God. This New Year can be your best year ever; allow yourself to experience what God can do for a man who will forget the past, including past achievements, past failures, past mistakes, past disappointments, etc. Receive that which eyes have never seen, nor ears ever heard and which has not entered into the heart of any man, as the things which God has prepared for them that love Him.

> *"Now you know what the Scripture means when it says, 'No eye has seen, no ear has heard, and no mind has imagined what God has prepared for those who love him.'"*
> **- 1 Corinthians 2:9** (NLT)

Today, you may be complaining about your spouse, children, lost opportunities, friends, etc., using such excuses for your condition. You may be thinking that everyone is overtaking you and *"when will it be my turn?"* Such gestures do not guarantee your change. Therefore, stop complaining about others and quit your excuses to God. The truth is, God is bringing about a change in you. To embrace it, you have to put the experiences of last year (both negative and positive) behind you; learn the lesson God wants you to learn from them, and take the necessary steps. Behold, God wants to do a new thing in your life – can't you see it? Don't build a monument on your past success; forget the past. Believe in God for a better future; don't give up, even when it seems nothing is happening. Keep working it out. It is not over until God says it is over. God does not lie.

"But these things I plan won't happen right away.
Slowly, steadily, surely, the time approaches when the vision
will be fulfilled. If it seems slow, do not despair,
for these things will surely come to pass. Just be patient!
They will not be overdue a single day!"
- Habakkuk 2:3 (The Living Bible: Paraphrased)

If you can hold on, your change will come. Hold on to Jesus, the Author, and Finisher of your faith. To maximize your divine opportunity, you must learn from your past and let it go!

Chapter 9

Cultivate "Good Habits" over "Bad Habits"

Habits are powerful. They are products of our early education, culture, religion, or practice.

*W*e are all creatures of habit, irrespective of the profession we practice, whether as a Minster, Medical Practitioner, Civil Servant, etc. Your habit determines what becomes of you. Hence, you must identify your negative habits so you can work on them.

What you are today is the culmination of many years of a continuous repeat of various habits. As such, you may have also cultivated some undesirable behaviours that people around you may have complained to you about. Though you argue it with them, within you, you know they are right with their observation or conclusion on you. You may have also been convicted about these behaviours or habits by the Spirit of God through the preaching of the Word. The fact remains that, the power of the gospel of our Lord, Jesus Christ, is potent enough to break bad habits if you can believe and yield to it.

One of the deadliest and most common habits is gossiping or whispering things about other people. The Bible declares:

> *A forward man soweth strife: and a whisperer separateth chief friends.* - **Proverbs 16:28**

As the Scripture says, gossip is usually started by a dishonest and uncaring person and it can destroy even the closest of friendships. When you engage in gossip, even if you are not the one who started it, you are showing yourself to be untrustworthy.

> *A gossip betrays confidence,*
> *but a trustworthy person keeps a secret.* - **Proverbs 11:13.**

As much as this Scripture warns against gossip, it also gives you reason not to engage in gossip. You will therefore be wise enough to not only abstain from the act of gossiping but also to frown at it when anyone comes to you with it. In this vein also, the Bible warns against any association with a gossip.

> *A gossip betrays confidence;*
> *so avoid anyone who talks too much.* - **Proverbs 20:19.**

It is very easy to be caught in the trap of gossip. When someone approaches you with information about someone else, consider whether you are part of the problem or the solution needed before making any contribution. If you realize you are not part of the problem nor the solution needed, then you don't need to listen to the story or else you would have joined that person in the gossip. It is better therefore that you stay away from the talebearer; politely tell him/her that you believe it is not something you need to know.

When you feel the urge to spread gossip, consider how the person concerned (as the subject of the gossip) would feel if he/she were right there in your midst during the conversation. If your words will tear someone down or even tarnish his/her reputation, ask the Holy Spirit to help you keep your mouth shut. The Bible says when you spread gossip (slander) you are a fool.

> *Whoever conceals hatred with lying lips*
> *and spreads slander is a fool.* - **Proverbs 10:18.**

This is how deadly a slanderer or gossiper is; his lies and gossip are only motivated by hatred in his heart, which he is not making known to those he gossips too. Thus, he destroys and murders a fellow with the words of his mouth.

Whatever your habit and how much it is destroying your character, integrity, personality, ministry, or marriage, you can overcome it, only if you can acknowledge the power of redemption that is in Jesus Christ.

Jesus can break the power of repeated sins and set you free from the prison of sin and death; He is the Master in the art of changing lives and yours can't be an exception. Stop playing games with your life!

If you are going to make the most of your opportunity, you have to first quit your negative habits and cultivate the good ones. It's a matter of choice and decision. If you choose to quit your bad habits and cultivate good ones, you will be disciplined about it.

Some of the negative habits in us have degenerated into a familiar spirit; you will need to lay hold on the power of God to free you from them.

Christ promised you a new life if you can accept Him as your Lord and Saviour. The moment you make that decision, the Holy Spirit comes to dwell in you to regenerate your spirit and give you the new life of Christ, which permeates your entire being and you become a new creature with the power to overcome your bad habits. As you allow Him to fill you with Himself, He also produces the Christ-like character, which is described as the *"Fruit of the Spirit"* in you, and with this, you can cultivate good habits in you that will portray you as a true Christian.

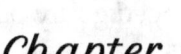

Chapter 10

Dissociate from "Ungodly Relationships"

If you walk with the wise, you will become wise;
the companion of fools shall be destroyed.
*- **Proverbs 13:20***

What role did the people you had a business, social interactions, and spiritual relationships with play in your life last year? If you will not waste this New Year again, you need to get rid of relationships that added nothing significant to you. Disengage from wrong leadership, business, or social relationship. You also need to break ties with zero people because zero people will only reduce you to nothing.

> *If you walk with the wise, you will become wise; the*
> *companion of fools shall be destroyed.*
> **- Proverbs 13:20**

Everyone who has achieved some sort of success will tell you that some people played certain roles in their pathway to success. Those who have ruined their lives will also tell you that there were people who influenced them negatively.

For you to succeed, you need godly people in your life that will bring out the best in you; they are people who will encourage you, fire you up, teach you, advise you, challenge you, chastise you, and help you to maximize your divine opportunity. The Bible says:

> *Iron sharpens iron, and one man sharpens another.*
> **- Proverb 27:17**

Deliberately and prayerfully enter the right relationships. Let God lead you to people who have what you lack; like those who are strong in areas where you are weak. Interact with those who have overcome what you are still battling with, and those who will add value to you. You need such friendships, business associations and spiritual relationships to be motivated and make a difference in life.

The Lord is sending you a new wine and new oil; you must be sensitive to them as God brings them to you in strategic partnerships and alliances. These people may not look like you expected; it might even be someone you really don't want to talk to, but God wants to use them to take you to your next level and that's why you need them. Whether you like them or not is not important; what is important is the good thing that God wants them to add to you, and you need to see them in that light.

Everybody needs a relationship but not just any kind of relationship. Godly relationships will contribute to your success whereas ungodly relationships hinder you from success. What we all need, therefore, are the right and godly relationships that will make an impact in our lives and God-given assignments. Such relationships will help to move you ahead to accomplish your purpose and attain the satisfaction of success in all that you do. With the right relationships in your life this New Year, you can make the most of your divine opportunities and take advantage of what the year holds for you.

Chapter 11

Be "Resolute"

Do not waste this year like you probably did in the past years.

If care is not taken, the days of the year will gradually roll by and the year will suddenly come to an end to usher in another New Year. As this continues to happen, you are getting older and closer to your grave.

Sincerely, when you look at yourself in the mirror, it may not look like you are growing old, but the reality is that every single moment you procrastinate or delay to take a step or action about your forgotten project or dream, you are not making the most of your God-given opportunities but only wasting your time and life.

Anything worth achieving takes time. As an infant, you crawled before you could walk. If you play a musical instrument, you will agree that it takes time before you mastered it. It is the same with pursuing your dream; you cannot accomplish everything in one night. Therefore, persevere and not despair; you are one step closer to manifesting your dream.

When my grandmother died, I had to relocate to the city with my parents, where I continued schooling. I was supposed to continue in the 5th Grade but due to the Nigerian educational system then and the fact that I came from the village to the city, which made my standard of education lower than expected; they dropped me back to the 3rd grade. This brought a setback for me such that, by the time, my age mates had graduated from middle to High school, I was just getting started in middle school. To make matters worse, I had to repeat my final year in High School because I did not have enough credits to secure college admission. Consequently, I had to wait another two years while trying to pass my West African Examination/GCE Exam. By the time I was ready for college, most of my age mates had finished their first degree or were in their final year in the university.

Following my academic setback, I gave up my dream of pursuing higher education because I could not imagine myself sitting in a classroom and being taught by my age mates who may have become lecturers in college. What I thought was best for me then was to simply give up furthering my education and pursuing my dream. Being ashamed of going to school, I found solace in Church activities. I got myself involved in so many Church activities to the extent that nothing mattered to me any more than ministerial activities and music.

But later on, intervention came for me, during a 7-day marathon fasting and prayer (no food and water), at the Basiribasiri Mountain in Akure. I still remember, vividly, the exact location and time the man of God, Pastor Famuyide called me; he said, "Moses" and I answered, "yes sir." "Sit down", was the instruction he gave me. Then, he asked me, "What are you doing now; what is your plan for the future; what is your plan to continue your education?" I really could not respond. So, he went further to say, "Listen to me brother, all the leaders of this association that you see now, did they go to school or not?" I answered, "They did." He continued, "Where are their children?" I answered, "In school." Then, he asked, "Why are they (the children) not here?" "Because they are in college," I replied. Afterward, he placed his hand on my shoulder and said, "Look at me and listen; if you do not pursue your education and dream, you will still be on this mountain praying and fasting when the children of all these leaders would have finished and returned from the university to become Pastors, Doctors, or Professors; then, you will be the one that will clean their chairs and sweep their floors for them, despite being older than them. If at all, they like you because they remember your good work, they will employ you to be their driver or gatekeeper in the house. "The choice is yours", he added, "I know you have given up and I know you are frustrated, but what you do not know is that the world is anxiously waiting for the glory that is about to be revealed in you." Thereafter, he just walked away.

Brethren, you can imagine what my feeling was at that instance! I sat down, looked at myself, and said to myself, "Moses, rise up, and pick up your dream again. The world is waiting for your manifestation." That was the end of the fasting and prayer. I went home and picked up my certificate. In fact, I was angry with myself for giving up and became desperate to take the next step as I was now ready to conquer any mountain. I prepared to fight for my dream and I did and because I did, I won. To God be the glory! He is faithful; He granted me success beyond my wildest imagination. Today, I have a double Master's degree in my chosen fields of study, and I am currently working on my doctoral degree. Thanks to the men of God, like Pastor Famuyide, who saw God's greatness in me and woke me up from my bed of frustration. Brethren, read my story, learn from it, and challenge yourselves to fulfill your destiny.

One summer in 1997, I met Pastor Adenodi in New York; during the Sunday morning service, after the praise and worship, he called me out and said, "Moses, your anointing oil is in Maryland." Honestly, I looked at him and said, "You can't be right as nothing can move me out of New York."

Incidentally, the following winter, I found myself divinely relocated to Baltimore, Maryland, according to the prophecy from the man of God. On my second night in Baltimore, I learned that Prophet (Dr.) Obadare was in town; so I went there to see him. The prophet was preaching when I walked in, but as soon as I sat down while praying, I heard my name. The Prophet said, "There is a young man here, by the name Moses Adedipe; come out" Being amazed, I said, "oh my God, what have I done again?" Then, reluctantly, I yielded to the call and walked towards the altar; upon which, he commanded me to kneel and I slowly knelt down. Brethren, right there, I was ordained as an Evangelist to be assisting the Senior Pastor, (Pastor Omolola), by the man of God, Prophet (Dr.) T.O Obadare. In 1974, He was also used by God to baptize me and I received a new name, 'Moses'.

You see; when you walk in the way of the Lord, His plan for your life will surely come to pass, no matter what.

Several months later, as I was driving my taxi cab in Baltimore, singing and praising God, the Holy Spirit spoke to me and said, "Go back to CAC Vineyard of Comfort, for I have a special assignment for you." It was not quite 10 minutes later when I received a call from Prophet (Dr.) Abiara, Papa, and he said, "Moooose, where are you? Take off your shoes and follow me." That was how I reconnected with Pastor (Dr.) David Adenodi and his beautiful wife, Evangelist Esther Adenodi, "Mama Moroti," at the Christ Apostolic Church, Vineyard of Comfort. Lanham, Maryland.

At the time when things got tough and I didn't know what to do or where to go, Pastor Adenodi and his wife were there for me and my family. I remember Pastor Adenodi once preached a sermon in early 1999/2000 titled, "*New You, New Life.*" He said, "The bottom is too crowded, the middle is too tight, and the only option you have is to be above." This statement sticks with me up till today; it awakened the giant in me to continue to fight for my dream. You can see how God has placed people in my path to help me to get to where I am today.

The fact remains that, no one can claim to have become whatever he/she is today by his/her own strength alone. God has, at certain points in time, sent the right helpers to you to uphold and direct you in your walk of destiny. My appreciation goes to these men of God for their love and their support for me and my family. Brethren, I declare to you today that it is not over until God says it is over and because God has not said it is over, you can't give up now!

> *"Teach us to realize the brevity of life,*
> *so that we may grow in wisdom"*
> - **Psalm 90:12** (NLT)

How long does it take for 365 days to be exhausted? The days fly away fleetingly. When are you going to start that project or the dream you've envisioned for years? When are you going to resume the projects you started but abandoned? Be resolute! Pursue your God-given dream and Jesus will make this year a significantly different year for you. Start with the first step and move on consistently, step by step, and your progress will be visible to all. If you do nothing about that new project, it will remain on the drawing board forever. Start with the little you have and start from where you are. If you expect a perfect condition before you start, you will wait for eternity.

> *"He who observes the wind will not sow;*
> *and he who regards the clouds will not reap"*
> *- **Ecclesiastes 11:4** (NKJV)*

According to NLT,

> *"Farmers who wait for perfect weather never plant. If they*
> *watch every cloud, they never harvest"*
> *- **Ecclesiastes 11:4***

There is no perfect time to achieve God's purpose for your life; you must be determined just to fulfill it, despite all the obstacles. If you wait for a perfect time, you will wait forever. To make the most of your divinely given opportunity, you must fight for your dream and start or resume the dream God has given you today and not tomorrow!

Chapter 12

A Good "Financial Plan"

When writing this book, I thought of the thousands of unique and godly people with God-given abilities, who never got a chance to live their lives to their fullest potential because they spent their entire lives chasing money.

They were more concerned about solving their financial problems and this kept them distracted from fulfilling their divine assignment. Some were focused on their divine assignment, but because they spent so much time struggling and worrying about money, they were not successful in their assignments.

Recalling previous years, most of the challenges you faced were probably money related and thus you were easily distracted. Therefore, it is easy to predict that, when the money problem is resolved, you will have wonderful peace of mind. That is because you worry less about money when you have plenty of money. Consequently, your mind becomes free to think meaningfully. This interpretation also means you are not truly free as long as you are not financially free; the reason being that you will always be obsessed with your financial needs in your mind. This goes on to rob you of the time and energy you would have dissipated towards being devoted to God, your dream, and your family. Your freedom from this quagmire only begins with the awareness that it is the will of God to prosper you because this changes your attitude and gives you positive behavior toward your own success in life. The Bible says:

> *"11 For I know the plans that I have for you,'*
> *declares the LORD, 'plans for welfare*
> *and not for calamity to give you a future and hope.*
> *12 'Then you will call upon me and come and pray to me, and I*
> *will listen to you."* - **Jeremiah 29:11-12**

God wants everyone to prosper and He has given us all the ability and the power to prosper!

"His divine power has given us everything we need for a godly life through our knowledge of him who called us by his own glory and goodness" **- 2 Peter 1:3**

Prosperity begins with understanding our role as God's stewards. Our lives, talents, abilities, and living in a world of unparalleled opportunities are all gifts from God. Even though His divine power has given us everything we need, we can only realize it on the basis of our knowledge of the divine power and how to cause it to manifest in our lives.

To maximize and make the most of every opportunity set before you this year, you must not leave your finances to chance. Plan your finances, including your income and your expenditure. In addition, pay attention to Scriptures that center on how God has given us the ability to prosper and make them the meditation of your heart; they will give you a good insight and clear revelation to becoming prosperous and a good steward of your Father in Heaven.

Furthermore, you will have to also learn to make your faith work for you; belief so much in your talent that you can engage it profitably to increase your income. Think about a legitimate business that you can do to increase your income. Also, take up a part-time or small business with which you can generate your gas, electricity, and cell phone bills.

The fact you must acknowledge is that you are not growing younger but older, and as you grow older, your financial obligation increases nearly every month and unless your finances increase proportionately to meet those legitimate demands, you will come under intense financial pressure. This pressure has the capacity of pushing you into debt and thereby reducing the quality of your life and also incapacitating you from doing things that are important to your life.

Plan to make more money legitimately through business ventures and wise investments. Look inward and find out what skills and talents you have that you can commercialize. Most importantly, stay under God's blessing and open the heavens by obeying the Word of God as you also fulfill your financial obligations to God.

Avoid impulsive and compulsive purchases, buying things on credit, especially incurring debts for consumption and not for investment. Don't buy things because they are cheap; buy only because you need them urgently. Be wise to count the cost of maintenance on products that may be higher than the purchase price. Avoid spending the money you don't have to buy what you don't need. This is a wise financial counsel. To make the most of your divine opportunity, you must manage your finances wisely and Godly. If you are interested in getting to know more about financial planning or product, Get started with companies like People Helping People (www.myphpdream.com) or www.Goasknewton.com. I also recommend the following books to you:

'Perfect Storm' by Patrick Bet-David
'Doing the Impossible' by Patrick Bet-David
'Tax-Free Retirement' by Patrick Kelly Titled.

Make sure you read my book too,
'CONQUERING YOUR GIANT - FEAR"

Chapter 13

Personal "Development"

What would you say was added to your life last year apart from material possessions, like clothing, shoes, jewelry, etc.?

In what ways did you improve yourself spiritually, mentally, or intellectually? Since you gave your life to Jesus Christ, how many times have you read the books of the Bible; how many good books did you study to increase and upgrade your knowledge financially and spiritually last year? What new skills have you acquired? What training have you undertaken?

If you are going to make use of every opportunity set before you by God this year, you must invest in yourself to upgrade mentally or intellectually. Make a necessary effort to build capacity for better performance and improvement in your career or business and life generally. I will advise you to join the People Helping People book club (*www.myphpdream.com*) or be part of the Zero Hour Family Book club (*www.zerohourfamily.org*) or (*www.CampofGod.org*)

What special skills or training are you planning to acquire this year? In what ways do you plan to invest in your self-development? We live in a high-tech knowledge age; you cannot afford to be ignorant of what is going on around you. Many do not even watch the news. How many times last week did you stop for a moment and tune in to a radio station just to listen to what is going on? You have cultivated the habit of listening to both the godly and ungodly junk and demonically possessed music in and out of your home but not having time for what can keep you abreast of current happenings.

If you want to fulfill your destiny, you must learn how to discipline yourself. Don't get me wrong! I do not mean you should deny yourself of having fun with your family and loved ones. Don't be too holy to have fun; go to the park and the movies with your children; enjoy your spouse, and spend quality time together. I told my wife, "*There is one thing I don't want to regret when we get to heaven.*" she asked, "*what is it*"? I answered, "*I don't want to get to heaven and regret that we did not have fun or enjoy each other enough on earth.*" She laughed!

Knowledge, skills, and expertise are everywhere and they are easy for you to acquire. But it takes understanding, foresight, and appreciation of the future benefits derivable from them for you to be motivated and willing to pay the price to acquire them.

"Wisdom shouts in the streets. She cries out in the public square. She calls to the crowds along the main street, to those gathered in front of the city gate: 'How long, you simpletons, will you insist on being simpleminded? How long will you mockers relish your mocking? How long will you fools hate knowledge?"
- Proverbs 1:20 – 22 (NLT)

Fools hate knowledge. Don't be a fool. It may be that you have to enroll for another degree or some advanced degree programme, computer literacy training, language training, driver's training, or apprenticeship in any trade and so on. Don't just talk about it, go and do it. This can enhance your marketability, improve your outlook or help in moving you in the direction of a career change that you are persuaded you need.

Be aware of the future of the industry you are operating in as it is constantly moving forward. Do whatever you need to do to stay on top of your career. It will cost you both time and money, yet, the benefits are invaluable.

Don't let this year pass you without learning something new that will contribute to your life significantly, both spiritually and mentally. Think about investing and starting a career that gives you a stream of income, whether you are there physically or not.

If you don't improve yourself or invest in your family, you will soon become obsolete and eventually irrelevant. Then, the money you think will always be there will stop coming to you. Remember, legitimate money comes to you only because you are solving a problem or meeting a need.

Chapter 14

Family "First"

I remember sitting down with one of my Pastor friends, trying to explain the importance of family protection and Life Insurance to him; after 35 minutes, he said, "Pastor, the Bible says, "I shall not die, but live to declare the glory of God." I simply answered, "Amen" to his declaration.

Then he said further, "I don't believe in Life Insurance. When I die, my wife, children, and the American government may leave my corpse to rot in the room if they like; I don't care. I did not inherit anything from my father. I have tried my best by bringing my family to America. If they like, let them bury me; whatever they want to do with me when I die is their business."

Reacting to his conclusions, I asked him, "*Do you have any car insurance?*" "*Yes*", he answered. I went on to ask him, "Do you have homeowner insurance?" "*Yes*" was his response from him. At this juncture, I asked him, "*Do you close your eyes when you drive?*" "*No*", he said. Then, I was prompted to ask him, "what is your response when the Bible says, "*a wise man will leave an inheritance for his children's children?*" He was quiet. So I continued, "You just bought a new Toyota Sienna on credit for your wife; you are still paying the car note on your Honda Accord, and you're still paying your mortgage regularly? Very soon, your twins will go to college. Meanwhile, your wife only works as a CNA (*Certified Nursing Assistant*), which earns her only $10.00 per hour and you are the breadwinner of the entire family here in the United States and in Nigeria. What if anything happens to you today? Then, both cars, which you bought on credit, will be repossessed; your home will be foreclosed, and your children will not be able to go to college anymore because your wife's income will not be sufficient to sustain the family.

At this point, he could not look at me face-to-face; suddenly, he looked up and said, well! The pastor will have to pray about protecting my family's future. I became so angry, and said, 'What a foolish and selfish Pastor you are!' The Bible says, "*a foolish man builds his house on the sand*" in the same vein, I went on to ask him, "Pastor, when you wake up in the morning, do you go to the mountain to pray about the type of clothing you need to put on, or the type of food you need to eat, or the type of shoes to wear, or maybe you should take a shower or not?" Rather, you just wake up to do all those things without consultation with the Holy Spirit because they are necessary.

Lamentably, because of his foolishness, I said to him, "Why are you so myopic, wicked, selfish, arrogant, and ignorant, even with a doctorate degree at the back of your name?" I told him frankly, "I cannot be your friend because you are selfish." The wife was crying like a baby. But later, she went ahead to undertake protection for the children and her future. What a smart and virtuous woman that builds her house with wisdom! Later on, she confessed to me that, "no one has ever talked to her husband like that" and I responded, "If a Pastor cannot be honest with a fellow Pastor, then we will have a problem and a query to answer to in heaven."

Sad to say, many people don't think about protecting and investing in their family because of their wrong priorities.

Many are so selfish and ignorant that they never think about tomorrow; they only think about themselves and fail to plan for their family. That's why things are upside down in their families. They believe life is all about them and so fail to set their priorities right with their families; they do not care about investing time and resources in their wives and children. Be wise! Invest the resources God has given you in your family. Don't be an absentee husband or wife;

your children need you at home this year. Don't be a workaholic or an outgoing socialite, who abandons the home. If you won't have time for your immediate family (spouse and children), then you should not have married! But since you are already married, God demands that you prioritize your time for your family. Your success at work can never compensate for your failure at home.

Your children and wife, or husband all need your time, both in quality and quantity. No amount of wealth that you acquire or the fame you have will do for your marriage and children should you lose them for your lack of love and attention.

I left Nigeria when my son was just 30 days old. As he grew up to boyhood, I was not there. My absence in his life was so miserable for him that he looked forward to my return daily. According to my wife, whenever he sees an aircraft, he will shout and say, "My Daddy is inside the plane; please come down, Airplane! Let my daddy come down". How he longed for a fatherly figure in his life at such a tender age!

I remembered, also, a story my sister-in-law told me once. She said there was a day, her last son misbehaved and she threatened her son that she would report him to his father, who would whip the daylights out of him that day when he comes home. On hearing this, she said, my son interrupted her and said, "Mummy, it is ok; he is lucky. At least, his daddy is coming home soon but my dad is living inside the airplane; he never comes home."

When my son finally came to join me in America, he was already 9 years old. Consequently, relating with each other at our reunion was a huge struggle for both of us. I had such great expectations for him; all I wanted from him was to be the best, well-behaved, and godly child. But what I did not know was that he would have to struggle to adjust and balance between the two cultures he was now getting exposed to and this was hard for him as he was trying to define and discover himself within that environment. I was completely ignorant of what had been going on in his life for years. Nonetheless, I love him so much and my goal for him was to be the best for God, at school, and home. But seeing that he was not holding up to my expectations, I became angry and disappointed. Yet, I never made the time to be with him or even spend some quality time to get to know him, review his homework, go to the park with him, or have fun with him. Rather, my schedule was always from home to work; then from work to school, and from school to Church. This was my daily routine: no fun, no games, no family time, nothing! I never even had time to attend any of his school programs. What made the relationship worse was the visible unjustified and unnecessary persecution experienced in the Church that I devoted all my life to and had robbed me of quality time with my family. Unfortunately, all my children were part of this ordeal. They witnessed everything without saying a word. They listened to all the conversations between me and my wife and heard what people were saying but thank God, they knew the truth, even though they were very young.

At this juncture, let me warn you that, if you are a Pastor and going through some persecution, be careful what you say and how you express your frustration and pain before your children. If you are members of the Church or a leader, beware of your actions, and what you do in the Church of God because the children are watching. Either for good or bad, they are watching you. My son in particular stored up all the frustrations, joy, persecution, hunger, fear, and anger inside him up until the time he left home and went to college.

After observing and seeing some strange actions in this my son, my eyes were opened and I realized that, if I didn't do something, I would lose my only son to the world and he may never return to the faith of believing in Jesus Christ again. He had become insensitive to Jesus and what we stood for as a family because of my mistakes and that of selfish, position-driven leaders in the Church.

Unfortunately, the situation at that time did not seem to favour my decision to work on my son; to see that he was restored to the faith and the time seemed too late for me because he was no longer at home but in the college and would only need to come home occasionally. But I thank God for His divine plans and for helping to fix what would have been a bad story. While in college, God, in his graciousness, caused my son to come across some Christian friends and he went with them to join another Church, for which also he stopped coming to our family church.

However, four years passed by, and one day he came home and said, "Dad, I am sorry; I do not see myself as Nigerian anymore. Secondly, I cannot be part of your Church as I cannot fit in with such a congregation; I simply do not belong there! I have my own Church family now." On hearing these words from my son, my head flew out of my neck; I nearly fainted. I was devastated and my wife and I cried unto God daily. I remember moments when my son and I would talk and argue about biblical issues from 8 pm to 4 am, all with the intention of getting to know his mind on biblical matters but the reality was that he had formed his own opinion already.

He had discovered who he wanted to be and it was to be independent. There was nothing I and my wife could do than to pray and advise him. With several prayers and patience, God finally intervened. Honestly, things are not as I would want them to be but Glory be to God in heaven, who has answered our prayers; things are now much better because the Lord is on our side. Our son has returned home now and he has even taken up the responsibility of leading the youths in the Church.

I have not told you this story in a bid to wash my dirty laundry in public but to make you learn from my life experience. I want you to invest precious and quality time with your family. The Church will always be there; God's work will surely continue, whether you are there or not. But you have only a limited time on earth with your family; make use of the opportunity and invest your best time in your family.

This year, you must search for your children that have run away from home and bring them back to the Lord; you must restore love in your family. Invest your God-given resources to redeem your family. Stop being an absentee parent; go back home from where you have wandered. Return to make a significant and indelible impact on your children before they leave you to start life on their own. Go back and cleave to your wife (or your husband). If the sweet wine has finished in your marriage, ask God to give you the new wine; just like Jesus did in the marriage of Cana of Galilee. It will become even sweeter. God is interested in your family and He will surely give you or bring peace to your troubled home. Amen!

Chapter 15

Appreciate your "Helpers"

I discovered a very interesting story in the Bible: the story of Moses and the seven daughters of the priest of Midian; it makes me realize how easy it is to forget the people who have helped us to get to where we are today.

It is so easy to make enemies of those whom God has used to help you. Yet, that doesn't change the fact that you did not get to where you are today by your sole effort, power, wisdom, or knowledge. You only got there because God placed some people along your pathway to help facilitate the journey for you. Despite this, many of us still fail to take cognizance of these people afterward. We do not remember even the name of our teachers in the college, not to mention the High School. We have completely forgotten their labour of love over us, which has helped to get us to where we are today.

Taking the experience of Moses as a case study, it gives us a clear picture of our subject matter. Moses had to run for his dear life into the desert when Pharaoh wanted to kill him. After enduring the cold and the heat of the wilderness for several days, he found himself resting by a well, hungry, tired, and weak. The Bible says:

> ¹⁵ *"When Pharaoh heard of this, he tried to kill Moses, but Moses fled from Pharaoh and went to live in Midian, where he sat down by a well.*
>
> ¹⁶ *Now a priest of Midian had seven daughters, and they came to draw water and fill the troughs to water their father's flock."*
> **- Exodus 2:15-16**

Despite being very weak and hungry, Moses found a reason to summon his strength and help these young girls fight the bullies and rebels that had made life miserable for them. I strongly believe that these girls had been going through this challenge for a long time. I am also of the opinion that due to this horrible challenge from these shepherds, these girls would have been hindered from completing their daily assignments and chores, as these shepherds would always delay them and drive them away. Affirmatively, the Bible says:

> *"Some shepherds came along and drove them away."*
> **- Exodus 2: 17**

The Job assignment they ought to finish, say like 3 hours, may turn out to take them the whole day, resulting from the delay of being driven away regularly from where God had divinely given them water for their families and their cattle. Perhaps, you are in the same situation, as it was with these seven girls, that, each time you want to accomplish a task, something will happen that will result in a delay for you. For instance, you dreamed of getting married at age 25 and now you are 35, going to 40 and still, there is no hope of a mate in sight. Or your colleagues and age mates have gone ahead of you achieving success, but a breakthrough is still far from you, as you are still struggling. Do not be discouraged. Today, I pray for you, in the name of Jesus Christ, that, every power and evil force that is causing delay along your way, driving your helpers away from you, and preventing you from your green pasture, the LORD will raise your Moses for you, who will fight your battle and make success easy for you. Amen!

It was not the first time that the shepherds would drive away these girls but, on this fateful day, God sent a helper, called Moses, who had traveled day and night, suffered many things in the wilderness, and now was divinely placed by the well of water for their help. Just at the nick of time, the girls came, as usual, to draw water and, once again, their enemies showed up but, praise God, their help was also at hand. The Bible says:

"Some shepherds came along and drove them away, but Moses got up and came to their rescue and watered their flock."
- Exodus 2:17

Oh, I pray that, at the right time, your helper will surely show up in Jesus' name. Moses rose up to the occasion, even though he was tired and it was not convenient for him, coupled with the fact that, he did not know the girls, which would have been a good reason not to interfere with their troubles but let them suffer alone, yet, because God had placed in his heart to help them, he came to their rescue. The Bible says:

"...But Moses got up and came to their rescue and watered their flock..." **- Exodus 2:17**

I pray that your helper will not be too late to rescue you in the name of Jesus. As soon as Moses helped these girls, the Bible says, they left Moses alone behind, in the wilderness, and went home to their father.

18 *"When the girls returned to Reuel their father, he asked them, "Why have you returned so early today?*

19 *They answered, "An Egyptian rescued us from the shepherds. He even drew water for us and watered the flock."*
- Exodus 2:18-19

How easy it can be to forget those who have been a blessing to your life! Many of us only turn out later to see the mistakes of our helpers but never think about their inconveniences and sacrifices for our sake in the past. We quickly forget them, ignore them, and reject them. Many of us will even go to the extent of speaking ill of them. We never want to see them anymore; they become bad people in our minds. Yet, when we were in trouble, they were there for us. I know this happens to Pastors a lot.

When we had no hope, they were there to support and give us hope. When we needed prayer, it was the Pastor. When we had a bad dream, the person to call was the Pastor. When there was trouble in the home, your Pastor was the next to call. When there was a challenge at work, or your children are misbehaving, you brought your Pastor in, even at midnight. Pastors never sleep; he prays for you and counsels you, even at the times they should be with their family. He stands to support you day and night, and now that the problem is over, peace has come, the marriage is settled, your spouse is back home, you have got the good job you desired and your children are doing fine because God has answered your prayers, should the pastor make a mistake, remember he is a human. Unfortunately, the next thing we do is, to start backlashing the pastor; he is not good, he is this or he is that. In fact, you even leave the Church and use the Holy Spirit as an alibi; claiming that, "the Lord is leading you to move forward" whereas you know that it is the flesh, your insensitivity or anger, that is leading you. You need to repent and go back to your Pastor and ask for forgiveness.

"The Prayer of the Righteous availeth much" - **James 1:27**

Do not forget your helper, no matter what he or she may do to you; always remember the good old days.

> *"And where is he?" Reuel asked his daughters.*
> *"Why did you leave him?*
> *Invite him to have something to eat."*
> **- Exodus 2:20**

God is asking you, today, "what have you done to appreciate your helper(s), where are they now, how many times have you sent a simple greeting card of $3.50 to appreciate your Pastor, that Prophet, or stranger that came as your helpers?" Thank God for Reuel, who asked them to go and bring Moses home, they would have left him in the wilderness to suffer and die there. Your helper might be in need of your help now; it is the right time for you to return the favour you received.

> ²¹ *"Moses agreed to stay with the man, who gave his*
> *daughter Zipporah to Moses in marriage.*
>
> ²² *Zipporah gave birth to a son, and Moses named him*
> *Gershom, saying, "I have become a foreigner in a*
> *foreign land." -* **Exodus 2:21-22**

What a way to reciprocate Moses' kind gesture. Hope revived in Moses, as a result, and he was now convinced enough to face the future with every sense of assurance in him.

Chapter 16

Be a "Blessing to Others"

*"If you think you are too important to help someone,
you are only fooling yourself.
You are not that important."*
Galatians 6:3 (NLT)

*I*t is good to be blessed but it is much better to be a blessing to others because the worth of a man is weighed by the good he does for others. One of the most common excuses for not giving to the needy is the thought that makes you say, "why can't they work too; after all, I worked hard for what I've got; so should they". But the Bible commands that we should bless others if we want to be blessed. God said to Abraham:

"I will bless you and make you a blessing,"
- Genesis 12:2

What God implies to Abraham here is, "I am going to pour a great blessing upon you such that even your mind will not be able to fathom it; however, the blessing is not for you only but for you to bless others so much so that they will know that you have a God who blesses people." This also comes to let you know that, you are not to keep the blessing of God to yourself nor live for yourself. It brings no Glory to God.

"Each one of us needs to look after the good of the people around us, asking ourselves 'How can I help'"
- Romans 5: 4 MSG

There is joy in being a blessing to others, even in the simplest way. If you live for yourself alone, you will die a small person but if you live to help others, your legacy shall never be erased. The life of a man is not valued by the abundance of his possessions but by how much impact and positive legacy he or she makes in the world before the zero hour. The founder of the Salvation Army, General Booth, said, "How can you convince a man of the Love of God if his feet are perishing with the cold?"

I have been led on many occasions by the Lord to talk about helping the needy, the orphans, and the widows and I have seen that there are times when many of us do not need to pray about the challenges we face because the solution could be, giving to others. We need to manifest the mercy of God by being merciful to receive mercy. Don't get me wrong! We need to pray about everything but most times, a heart of giving and rendering a helping hand to the needy will bring solutions to our situations in ways we cannot imagine.

If you find yourself amid a crisis and your prayers aren't being answered, you need to consider the charges that God gave the Israelites after they had fasted and prayed for 40 years without result. He says:

> 6 *"Is not this the kind of fasting I have chosen: to loose the*
> *chains of injustice and untie the cords of the yoke,*
> *to set the oppressed free and break every yoke?*
>
> 7 *Is it not to share your food with the hungry*
> *and to provide the poor wanderer with shelter —*
> *when you see the naked, to clothe them,*
> *and not to turn away from your own flesh and blood?*
>
> 8 *Then your light will break forth like the dawn,*
> *and your healing will quickly appear;*
> *then your righteousness[a] will go before you,*
> *and the glory of the Lord will be your rear guard.*
>
> 9 *Then you will call, and the Lord will answer;*
> *you will cry for help, and he will say: Here am I.*
> *"If you do away with the yoke of oppression,*
> *with the pointing finger and malicious talk"*
> **- Isaiah 58:6-9**

When you care for the needy, the Lord promises to "deliver you in time of trouble" (**Psalm 41:1**) and, I bet, you can take that to the bank.

You certainly cannot satisfy everybody but you can contribute to the lives of people around you and those you meet on your journey this year, according to your ability. It does not have to be money always; everybody can help someone else in some way or the other. There is always somebody you can help.

The Bible says it is more blessed to give than to receive. This should be your watchword. Those around you should be able to have a feeling of gratitude towards you, as the widows did towards Dorcas for her good deeds (**Acts 9: 36-43**).

Your life activities should not make everyone around you say, "Thank God you are dead; after all, when you were alive, you were of no good to your friends or your neighbors." When you bless people, God will bless you back in His own way. The Psalmist says:

> *"Once I was young, and now I am old. Yet I have never seen*
> *the godly abandoned or their children begging for bread.*
> *The godly always give generous loans to others,*
> *and their children are a blessing."*
> - **Psalm 37:25-26** (NLT)

Be a blessing to others this year; don't be selfish. There is always someone you can help. According to Pastor (Dr.)

David Jeremiah, in one of his messages on the radio, said, John Wesley is reported as having this as his motto: "Do all the good you can, with all the means you can, in all the ways you can, in all the places you can, at all the times you can, to all the people you can, and as long as you ever can." Whatever good you do to others, you are sowing a seed for yourself, which you shall reap one day or your children will surely reap one day.

Self-centeredness and stinginess hinder people from success. Selfishness is, manifesting a lack of love for others. Many Christians don't give; they are only concerned about themselves. Many give nothing more apart from the offerings and tithes in the Church. They close their eyes to the people they are supposed to be a blessing to. Yet the Bible says, the gift of a man (*spiritual, material, or financial*) will make room for him.

> "*A gift opens the way and ushers the giver into the presence of the great.*" - **Proverbs 18:16**

Generosity can open doors for you. It is this generosity that the world has abused and turned to bribery. The Bible condemns bribery as we have seen earlier, but it says a generous soul shall be made fat.

> "*A generous person will prosper; whoever refreshes others will be refreshed*" - **Proverbs 11:25**

Generosity pays. In **1 Samuel 30:8-19,** David was able to get the needed information that led to the recovery of all that the Amalekites had carried away because he was generous and kind to the starving Egyptian, whose master had abandoned him for being sick. Many Christians miss it because they think their Church giving, which has its reward too, is all that is needed and so they fail to take advantage of affecting, positively, the lives of those, who can be a blessing to them and help them to succeed. I am not talking about the kind of giving (bribery) that is done in the world, which is meant to manipulate the receiver. The Bible says:

"Whenever we have the opportunity, we should do good to everyone" - **Galatians 6:10** (NLT)

"Use every chance you have for doing good" - **Ephesians 5:16** (NCV)

"Whenever you possibly can, do good to those who need it. Never tell your neighbor to wait until tomorrow if you can help them now" - **Proverbs 3:27** (TEV)

The people you help may not necessarily be the ones that will repay you, and you shouldn't even expect them to repay you. God knows how to pay you back.

A servant of God rightly said, "Whatever you make happen for somebody, God will make happen for you". I agree with this God's servant, Zig Ziglar who said, "You'll always have everything in life that you want if you'll help other people get what they want" The secret is: don't live for yourself. God told me some years ago, "If you live for

106

yourself, you will die a small man" Don't die a small man; begin to give of yourself to people today. Some may abuse it, but many will appreciate it. In any case, you are not doing it for them to thank you but you are sowing a seed for yourself and you will reap it in due season if you faint not.

> *"Let us not become weary in doing good,*
> *for at the proper time, we will reap a harvest*
> *if we do not give up."* - **Galatians 6:9**

Let's balance the equation of doing good deeds and showing kindness to other people; you are not required to try to please everyone. It is not possible to please everybody. Helping others does not mean you compromise and bend in ways you shouldn't, just because you want them to see you as a nice person. That is what a lot of people do when they don't want to offend people. This is not right and the giver will end up compromising his/her faith and thus, putting his/her family finances in trouble.

No one is expected to carry the burden and problems of the entire extended family and neglect that of the immediate family. Your responsibility, as a Christian, is to provide first for your immediate family.

I listened to Charles Stanley on the radio one day and he said, "There is one guaranteed formula for failure, and that is to try to please everyone" You cannot satisfy everyone; you can only help as many people as you have the means to help. Do not be sentimental; do only what is right, and do only what you can afford to do. Don't go out deliberately to impress people so that they can speak well of you because not everyone will do that, even if you strip yourself naked to give to them. As you are trying to help somebody, another person will be unhappy about it, but you can't do anything about that.

Don't try to be a man-pleaser, but be a God-pleaser; help those you are in a position to help. The ones you are not in a position to help due to lack of means or because it violates the Word of God, don't have a guilty conscience about it. Even if helping them does not contradict the Word of God; when you do not have the means, don't be troubled about it. Helping that person may be an assignment for someone else. You can still encourage them and pray that God will use somebody else to help them. You cannot help everybody that comes your way. Paul the Apostle says:

> *"Am I now trying to win the approval of human*
> *beings, or of God? Or am I trying to please people? If*
> *I were still trying to please people, I would not be a*
> *servant of Christ".*
> **- Galatians 1:10**

Therefore, beware of eye-service or seeking the approval of men as you go about benevolent acts. Whatever you do to help others, let it be to fulfill the will of God as the servant of Christ.

Chapter 17

Be Expectant and "Grateful to God"

Thank God for the season of celebration that just ended; hundreds and thousands of turkeys died with so much to eat and drink, in the spirit of celebration and thankfulness.

However, the question is, did your gratitude last beyond your afternoon nap? For many, that's the extent of their thanksgiving; a one-time, get-it-out-of-the-way holiday that reminds them to reflect on how blessed they are. Too often and quickly, we resort to being ingrates; we forget what God has done and only remember to thank Him once a year. But God wants us to be thankful to Him at all times and for all things. The Bible says:

"In everything give thanks; for this is God's will for you in Christ Jesus." - **I Thessalonian 5:18**

Gratitude should come naturally to believers in response to all God has done on their behalf, but for our hardness of heart, God enjoins us with commands to give thanks always. So if you're saved, Spirit-filled, sanctified, submissive, and yet suffering, you have one thing left to do in order to follow God's will: be thankful to God, regardless of what you are passing through.

Apostle Paul instructed us that, in everything, we should give thanks; this allows believers no excuse for harboring ingratitude. Everything carries an unlimited requirement which refers to everything that occurs in life. With the obvious exception of personal sin, we are to express thanks for everything, and every time. No matter what struggles or trials we face, God commands us to find reasons for thanking Him always, no matter what the situation.

2 *"Consider it pure joy, my brothers and sisters, whenever you face trials of many kinds,*

3 *because you know that the testing of your faith produces perseverance"*
- James 1:2-3

The Apostles left the Sanhedrin, rejoicing because they had been counted worthy of suffering disgrace for the Name of Christ (Act 5:41).

The single, greatest act of worship you can render to God is to thank Him. It's the epitome of worship because, through gratitude, we affirm God as the ultimate source of both trials and blessings. With a thankful heart, you can say, in the midst of anything, *"God, I praise you."* If you're not obeying that command, you're not following God's will. Think of it like this: If gratitude doesn't come easy for you, neither will finding God's will. Or to put it another way: if you struggle with being thankful, you'll struggle with following God's will.

Rejoice in the Lord always and everything will be better than your past years and even beyond your expectation.

> *"Always be full of joy in the Lord. I say it again — rejoice!"*
> **- Philippians 4:4**

Secondly, we must have positive expectations. Positive expectation is not talking about a human philosophy or stressing the natural hope, but emphasizing a practice rooted in the Word of God, which cannot fail because the Word of God has a self-fulfilling ability. Your faith in God determines a lot of what you get from life. With your faith in God, you can change negative circumstances. With your faith in God, you can achieve your goals. Faith in God does not grumble in the face of discouragement; it knows that, though weeping may endure for a night, joy comes in the morning (**Psalm 30:5**). The Bible says:

> *All things are possible to him that believes....*
> *With God all things are possible.* **- Mark 9:23; 10:27**

111

Let your faith be in God through Jesus Christ alone. With God, you can climb every mountain before you this year. He will level the mountains for you and He will fill all the valleys. He will make all your crooked paths straight; He will steer your boat across the stormy sea and you will sail to the other side safely.

You must be ready to endure as you move into this year and despise all the shame. Let your eyes be on the reward, rather than regretting, fretting, lamenting, or grumbling like you probably did in past years; live a life of thanksgiving.

Count it all joy, regardless of what happens to you this year, and give thanks for everything. This is how to change your negative conditions and multiply your positive experiences. Give thanks to God for both the negative and the positive. Negative attitudes will only make you weary, but the joy of the Lord is your strength (**Nehemiah 8:10b**)

> *"Always be full of joy in the Lord.*
> *I say it again — rejoice!"* - **Philippians 4:4**

Thanksgiving comes with joyfulness. It is only when you are joyful that you can actually have the courage to give thanks, in spite of whatever happens. It is either you are joyful or grumble over your situation. Learn therefore to be joyful so you can be thankful. Don't let whatever you are going through take your joy from you.

Chapter 18

Appropriating Cautions and "Boundaries"

In the Physical world, boundaries are easy to see. There are fences, signs, walls, or hedges all around as physical boundaries.

Likewise, in the spiritual world, there are boundaries: these are harder to see but they exist. In reality, spiritual boundaries are there to increase your love and save your life.

Boundaries define our limits. They define what you can do and what you are not to do as well as where you will end and where someone else will begin. Boundaries help us to

113

distinguish our property so that we can take care of it. My parents in our local village used kola-nut trees and palm trees to define their farm or land boundaries.

Boundaries also help to differentiate you from someone else; we have differences in culture and nature.

God enacted the concept of boundaries; He defines Himself as a distinct, separate Being and He is responsible for Himself. He takes responsibility for His personality by telling us what He thinks, feels, plans, allows, will not allow, likes, and dislikes. Likewise, you must take responsibility for your personality; you must let people know who you are, what you think, feel, plan, allow, will not allow, like, and dislike.

God limits what He allows in His camp. He confronts sin and allows consequences for every behavior. He guards His house and does not allow any evil thing to come near. He only invites people who will love Him and do His will, and finally, He opens and closes the gate of His boundaries appropriately, according to the guidelines He has set to guard His boundaries.

We should be like God and not allow any junk and garbage in our hearts and our boundaries. Stop feeding your soul with junk from the world, especially junk music.

"Do not give dogs what is sacred; do not throw your pearls to pigs."
- Matthew 7:6

114

If you put what is precious to you around fools, they will trample them under their feet by casting it down in their speech and then tear it to pieces. The Word of God is telling you here to create a boundary in your heart. Keep the pearls inside and the pigs outside. As a Christian, you should be able to open up your boundaries and let the good in and the bad out. You need to open your gate and "let God in". God has something good to give us; some other people sent by God have good things to give us, and we need to "Open up to them" (**2 Corinthian 6:11-13**)

Boundaries help us to guard our hearts with all diligence and as we continue to make the most of our divine opportunity, we need to keep the things that will nurture us inside our fences and keep the things that will harm us outside. In short, boundaries help us keep the good in and the bad out, and that way, we guard our treasure.

> *"Then God said, "Let us make mankind in our image, in our likeness, so that they may rule over the fish in the sea and the birds in the sky, over the livestock and all the wild animals, and over all the creatures that move along the ground."*
> **- Genesis 1:26**

In the same way, God gave us His "*likeness*" and also a personal responsibility with limits. He wants us to "rule and subdue" the earth and to be responsible stewards for the life He has given us; to do that, we need to develop boundaries just like God has. Brethren, as you proceed on your life journey, some godly people will have good things to give to you, and you need to "open up to them".

> 12 *"We are not withholding our affection from you, but you are withholding yours from us.*
>
> 13 *As a fair exchange – I speak as to my children – open wide your hearts also."*
> **- 2 Corinthian 6:12-13**

Stop assuming that everybody hates you or that no one loves you or cares about you; you need to give people the freedom to help you.

If you will live your life according to what you have learned from Christ, then you must practice caution in your language; that is, "be slow to speak." Often, our mouth reveals what kind of a person we are. Be careful what you say!

You must practice caution in your display of anger if you will live like Christ and follow what you have learned from Him; be "slow to wrath." No good ever comes from a display of anger; be it in the home, at the office, in a church, or in a business meeting.

The course of Christ is being destroyed, and in serious damage, when the testimony of us displaying such anger in the presence of unbelievers, is recorded in heaven.

Chapter 19

Guard against "Disobedience"

¹ "If you fully obey the LORD your God and carefully follow all his commands I give you today, the LORD your God will set you high above all the nations on earth.
² All these blessings will come on you and accompany you if you obey the LORD your God:
³ You will be blessed in the city and blessed in the country."
- Deuteronomy 28:1-3.

The ultimate secret of a successful life is the level of obedience to the Word of God practiced. If you are willing and obedient you shall eat the best of the land.

God has released His blessings upon those who will obey His Word, and under these blessings, no man can fail. The simple fact is that the first hindrance to success in life is disobedience to the Word of God, which will bring a man under a direct curse from heaven. Who can help a man, whom God has cursed, to succeed? The opposite goes for the obedient: who will stand in the way of the success of a man whom God has blessed? In reality, show me a man that is succeeding in everything he does and I will show you a man that fears and obeys God.

The Bible declares that man must be willing to obey. God will not force obedience on anyone. (**Isaiah 1:19**).

> *"The doer of the word shall be blessed in what he does."* - **James 1:25**

Disobedience to God's Word brings a man under a curse and to be cursed means to be empowered to fail. A cursed man cannot succeed. No man can make it under the curses in **Deuteronomy 28:15-68**, which are direct consequences of disobedience to the Word of God.

From Genesis to Revelation, all the people that were blessed by God, in the Bible, were obedient to His Word; from Abraham, Isaac, Jacob, and Joseph, to Mary, etc. Your number one step towards success in life is to begin to obey the Word of God, for it is more efficacious and effectual than prayer. You can spend 10 years on the mountain, praying, prophesying, binding, and losing, but if there is an absence of the full knowledge of the Word of God and you are disobedient to His Word spoken to you, you are just wasting your time.

Prayer will never compensate for your disobedience. May I let you know that, you cannot get through prayer what you have lost by disobedience! Alternatively, you can get what you did not even ask for from God by simply obeying the Word of God. God honors His Word more than His name.

If you are not born again, you are disobeying the Word of God. That, in itself, is the highest disobedience on earth. God, out of His love, has given Jesus to die for you on the cross and He expects you to believe in Him, accept Him as your Lord and Saviour, and be saved.

Will you do that right now and start the process of opening up your life to divine blessing, under which you can't fail? What a great privilege you have now! Make the most of this opportunity now and settle with your Creator.

Chapter 20

Respect "Time"

Anyone who values life and time is someone who wishes to derive something special from it.

*L*ast year was full of boundless opportunities to do well, and to grow spiritually and intellectually but, unfortunately, many of us failed to manage time properly. God has given us 24 hours each day. This represents our time on earth for each day. It is amazing how people waste their time and indeed their lives by ignoring the importance of valuing time. What the majority of us do not know is that we are not just wasting our time, but we are wasting our lives, and the span of life wasted cannot be regained.

Those who don't have respect for their time cannot have respect for the time of other people. Time is supposed to be invested in what is profitable; what is useful for your life's assignment; what blesses people; what builds up and that which will make other people succeed. The majority of us waste so much time talking nonsense and doing nothing that, at the end of the day, we get angry when we do not accomplish much.

Many, due to their lack of time management always pay tithe to the Police Department. How you spend your seconds determines how you will spend your minutes, your hours, your days, your weeks, your months, and your years. By the end of the year, your age will have increased and then you will begin to complain that you are getting older, also with utterances like: "*I am tired, I am this and that*" without accomplishing anything. The fact is that you have wasted much valuable time talking about unnecessary things. You talked about other people's businesses, shoes, clothes, husbands, wives, and the list goes on. The Psalmist says:

> "*Teach us to number our days,*
> *that we may apply our hearts unto wisdom*"
> **- Psalm 90:12**

To succeed in life, you must use your time wisely. To maximize your divine opportunity, you need to manage your life well. As much as you need to spend time to show love to people, as commanded by God, beware of people who will waste your precious time. Resolve that you are not going to waste any more time (or your life) on anyone that seems unserious but be willing to help those who know where they are going and are ready to change.

During a counseling session, I sat with a brother for 2 hours, trying to diagnose his problem. God gave me the grace to narrow his challenges down to four points, which I wrote down and then I showed him the steps he needed to take to overcome these challenges. I prayed with Him and I told Him to go and do what we had agreed on. It was unbelievable that his next statement was: "Pastor, can you summon all the prayer warriors to come and pray for my deliverance?" Not understanding where 'he was coming from, I said, "Deliverance from what?" He answered, "Deliverance from all the problems we have been talking about." I stood up drained, and said, "My brother, you have taken from me 2 hours of my life, which you cannot give back to me neither can I gain it back but it is gone forever." Afterward, I went on to ask him, "Who is your pastor, and which Church do you pay tithe and offering?" In response, he gave me the name of the Church and it happened to be one of the "big Churches" in Houston. Then I said, "I will strongly recommend you go and call your Pastor to summon prayer warriors from your Church to deliver you from whatever is going on in your life. I have wasted 2 hours of my life to help you and you are not willing to take any step on all that I recommended". Amazingly, he said, "I don't know his number as I have never met him. I only see him on the stage and TV". Then I concluded, as I got up, "Thank you, brother, for visiting, God bless you and please have a wonderful day."

Know how to manage your time so that people, who are likely to waste your time, don't gate crash into your schedule or take more time than they deserve from you. Learn to manage one minute, one hour, then one day, and indeed your life. Thus, you show that time to you is a currency like money that is not to be wasted!

I believe that, if you will make use of your valuable time and get rid of all these hindrances in your life, you will succeed greatly by the kingdom's standards. Don't join the rat race; follow the Word of God. Let the Word of God be the benchmark for your belief and conduct. Fear God and keep His commandments for this is the whole duty of man.

Chapter 21

"Fear Not"

Now all has been heard; here is the conclusion of the matter;
Fear God and keep his commandment
for this is the duty of mankind."
Ecclesiastes.12:13

There are a lot of reasons that could be the cause for the delays that happen in our lives, but there is one that can always be traced to us and it is, fear. God says don't be afraid, but when something negative happens, the first thing we do, as our first reaction, is to always go against the instruction to *"fear not"* and we disobey God in that respect.

In **Exodus Chapter 13** and **Numbers Chapters 13-14**, fear was the first mistake the Israelites made as a nation. First, they were afraid before the Red Sea, and next, as they continued in their journey after God had crossed them through the Red Sea, they were afraid again to enter the Promised Land because of the walled cities and the giants that were there. They said:

> *"We are afraid... The people there are stronger and taller than we are and the cities are walled cities."*
> **- Numbers 13:28 (KJV)**

They had enough faith to move out of Egypt because they hoped for a better life, but when they saw trials, their faith was put to the test; they lost their faith for fear and the excitement for the Promise Land vanished as a result. They were not able to trust God enough to move into the Promised Land, for which they left Egypt in the first place.

Indeed, fear is the greatest obstacle to happiness, peace, and fulfillment at any level, whether personal, national, or international. *Anger, hatred, prejudice, aggression, violence, and war* can also ultimately be attributed to fear. Definitely, fear is the Mother of all *'Negative Emotions'*.

From the moment we get out of the security of our mother's womb, we experienced separation and, immediately, were subjected to various forms of fear.

I wrote specifically on this subject in a book titled, "War Against Fear" and I encourage you to get a copy to get your victory over fear and be that child that God will be pleased with.

While I was growing up in my father's village, in Africa, at certain times of the day, my parents would not let us out of the house because they believed there were some terrible spirits out there that might harm us; so they'd make sure we stayed indoors because they were afraid something might happen. This is what living in fear actually means.

Listen carefully! Our enemy, Satan, specializes in using fear as a tool, and this should not be so with you. He sends the spirit of fear to grip us and then he uses it to entrap and enslave us because we lack the knowledge of how to dismantle this manipulation. You must understand that God has not given us the spirit of fear, but of power; therefore, the spirit of fear has no power over us. I pray that by the time you finish this book, you will have regained your freedom from fear in Jesus' name.

Fear is a spirit. That's why the Bible talks about the spirit of fear. As a spirit, fear takes possession of people. Once it takes possession of you, it gains dominion over your life and makes you its slave. It will take Christ for you to be free from the slavery or bondage of fear and that happens when you make Christ your Saviour and Lord because He sends the Holy Spirit to indwell your heart.

126

Fear is a common experience for all. While there are people who can handle snakes like toys, others, like me, become scared stiff just at the sight of snakes. For instance, if during a Sunday morning service, someone suddenly raises an alarm about a snake being in the sanctuary, the majority will scamper out to safety. The chance may have it that many of us will probably stop coming to Church because a snake was killed in the Church, irrespective of our spirituality. The real root of the problem is that we are afraid of snakes and such fear can magnify the situation and cause it to grow into a monster in our hearts, which may impact our lives in many ways.

The truth is that, if you have an understanding of what you are afraid of, you can easily overcome it. Fear is simply false evidence that appears to be real. Therefore, whenever you are afraid of anything, remember that it could be false evidence that appears to be real. No wonder Jesus says, concerning the devil:

"You belong to your father, the devil, and you want to carry out your father's desire, he was a murderer from the beginning, not holding to the truth, there is no truth in him. When he lies, he speaks his native language (What is natural to him): for he is a liar and the father of lies"
- **John 8:44**

There are four major points as golden nuggets I'd like to share with you from this passage.

> First, "The devil is a liar and father of Lies".
> Second, "The Truth is not in him".
> Third, "he uses falsehood to deceive God's people into fear."
> Fourth, "his natural language is deceit and lies".

This has given me a special definition for fear, as: "**FALSE EVIDENCE - APPEARING REAL**"

On the flip side, remember the following truths about God from the same Scripture, **John 8: 44**:

> God is not a Liar
> He is also the father of all Truth
> The truth is in Him
> He uses Faith to bring Freedom to His people
> His natural language, (His mother's tongue) is Truth and Righteousness

In the act of war, you can easily overcome your enemy if you have his background information, know his weaknesses, and strengths, and keep up with his intelligence-gathering system. God, in His Word, exposed the nakedness of the devil more than two thousand years ago. Yet, many still subject themselves to the lordship of fear. The Bible says the author of your problem is a liar and the father of lies. Let me ask you a question: if God says someone is a liar, why are you still fearful of him and subject yourself to his control and manipulation?

God's Word says, there is no truth in what you see or perceive as a problem; there is no truth in what you see as failure; there is no truth in what you see as your sickness or disappointments; there is no truth in whatever the devil has deposited in your life that's making you believe you are miserable. You are only miserable because you have accepted the report of the enemy. Jesus said:

> *"I am the way, the truth, and the life;*
> *no one comes to the Father, except through me."*
> **- John. 14:6**

This means that only Jesus tells the truth because the truth is in Him as much as He is the truth. Listen, the truth about your situation is that, you are afraid where there is nothing to fear and your fear is why you cannot break through that barrier set before you by the devil. Come on, get on your feet, and bring down the barrier of fear in your life!

When fear roams freely in the city, the people are terror-stricken and are held hostage by their fears. This is what's going on right now in the United States. The fear of terrorism has totally changed the American way of life, and freedom is held captive. There seems to be a mounting fear of the unseen terrorist everywhere. That's what happens when we give room to fear; it quickly grows and muzzles our entire existence.

(GET A COPY OF
"CONQUERING YOUR GIANT - FEAR"
AND LEARN MORE ABOUT FEAR TODAY)

The problem with fear is that it keeps you in the wilderness; in the desert and barren places of life. It prolongs the delay. Fear and faith cannot live together in the same house. Many of your dreams have never been fulfilled, not because of God, but because of you. You can only receive from God by faith and yet you wouldn't step out in faith. God says don't fear. Fear causes delays in your life and keeps you from moving ahead.

The antidote to fear is to focus on God's presence. Take the joy of the Lord and let it fill you with the love of God.

> [18] *"But God led the people about, through the way of the wilderness of the Red Sea: and the children of Israel went up harnessed out of the land of Egypt....*
>
> [21] *And the LORD went before them by day in a pillar of a cloud, to lead them the way; and by night in a pillar of fire, to give them light; to go by day and night:*
>
> [22] *He took not away the pillar of the cloud by day, nor the pillar of fire by night, from before the people."*
> **- Exodus 13:18, 21-22**

Realize that God is with you. When you seem afraid of going after your God-given dream, you need to focus on God's power and His faithfulness. He says, "I will always be with you." There will never be a time in your life when God is not with you. He's with you now as He always has been and He always will be. He is with you on your good days and your bad days, as well. He's with you whether you feel it or not because He says, "I will always be with you."

By research, the expression, "fear not" is written 365 times in the Bible and there are 365 days in a year. This implies that each of the "fear not" in the Bible goes for each day of the year. God is saying, no matter what you are facing, don't be afraid. When God says, "Fear not, for I am with you," it is not for the purpose of positive thinking or motivational speech or for pulling yourself up by the psychological bootstraps but it is to stir your faith in Him.

You'll never face any situation in life if God isn't present with you; it's just that, you tend to easily forget that. Whenever you start becoming afraid, quickly focus on God's presence and let go of the fear. Learn to always stand strong on the conviction that God is with you all the time.

You may be in the delay phase right now. You've been praying for something and it hasn't happened yet. You are starting to think that God has forgotten you. God has not forgotten you. He knows what you're going through. It is a delay by design.

Remember that, faith nurtures faith and fear nurtures fear; therefore, place your trust in God. First of all, yield the little things in your life, then His love and wisdom will be revealed and confirmed to you; thereafter, with time, as you continue to yield to Him, the bigger things in your life will be under His control.

Put God to the test; even if it is only in the little things, you will soon find out that He is actively working on the big issues in your life. When this happens, fear will start to diminish until your whole life is free of destructive fear. Your life will increasingly be controlled by positive faith and will taste success above fear. Finally, remember that God wants to build your character and He wants you to learn to trust in Him. You can count on Him for His help. Make the most of your life and don't be afraid!

s

Chapter 22

Don't "Fret"

The events happening around us in the world, coupled with family challenges and responsibilities can have unsettling influences on our personal life.

When your lifestyle has to change as a result of changing circumstances, you will be filled with premonitions and uncertainties, but, behold, the Word of God admonishes you to, rest in the LORD, and wait patiently for him. If you desire not to be completely overwhelmed by anxiety and fear, you must cling in faith to the living Christ and derive your strength from Him.

Do not fret! To fret means to worry. The admonition of God's Word to you, therefore, is that you should not get worried about anything. Don't get uptight! Unfortunately, we do that when we get into delays. We worry, get uptight, and get stressed out. Worrying will only occupy you with the wrong thoughts and it will also cause you to be drained of your strength.

When you worry, you bind and push away the hands that can help you. God responds to faith and not to fear, which is laced with worries and stress. Learn to trust God in the delays you face. After all, it is God that is leading you. Regardless of whatever problem that is upsetting your personal life, look back over history; you will realize how, several times, you have struggled through difficult times, and yet the challenges never overcame you. God says, don't fret; don't worry; don't get uptight about the situation. We grumble when we're waiting for God to act and we think that He is being late in doing so. We are always too much in a hurry for the manifestation of God's answer. But this is what God's Word says about that:

"And he sins who hastens with his feet." - **Proverbs 19:2**

When we try to take matters into our own hands and try to help God out, we get in trouble. It's frustrating when we are in a hurry and God isn't. God is never in a hurry. The Bible says with Him, a day is like a thousand years, and a thousand years like a day. He's larger than time. One of the most useless things to try to do is to speed up God.

When you get impatient, you start trying to work it out yourself. For instance, when you get a dream from God, you zealously make the decision to go for it immediately.

Along the way, the delay comes and then the vision is no longer moving fast enough for you. You start trying to figure out ways of working out God's dream on your own. Then also, you start trying to force the issue.

Abraham did that. God said He was going to give Abraham a son. At 85, Abraham still didn't have one and Sarah was already incapable of conceiving. He decided to try an alternative; of having a child by Hagar, Sarah's handmaiden. Hagar got pregnant and bore a son. They named him Ishmael. Abraham thought he had the miracle child in Ishmael. Unfortunately, God said that Ishmael was not a miracle child. He wasn't the baby God said would be the miracle baby. God blessed Ishmael, anyway, and he also became the father of a great nation. He's the father of all the Arabs.

But God said He would surely give Abraham the promised child. Later, Abraham had Isaac through Sarah, who was way gone in years, and although she was not able to have a child at the time most women conceive, she had her baby at a grandmother's age. Isaac became the father of the Jewish nation. You know what that means, judging from the unrest created against Israel by the Arab nations that surrounded them.

Learn not to fret, but trust God's timing. The Bible says:

> *"Rest in the Lord, wait patiently for Him to act."*
> **- Psalm 37:7-8**

Don't fret and worry; it only leads to harm. Resting in God is an act of faith and it includes trusting God's timing. It means you must wait on God.

At one time, Jesus and the disciples were in a boat and Jesus fell asleep. A big storm came up and the disciples freaked out. Jesus was in the corner of the boat sleeping. They frantically woke Jesus up, saying, "Why are you sleeping?" Now, did they think God was going to let the boat sink with Him in it? Jesus, by His sleeping, was saying: I trust God, my Father, to keep us safe even in the middle of a storm. I don't have to worry about it.

When we get into a storm, we lay awake all night and fret about it. The very fact that we're lying awake at night means we're not living by faith. We can't get any sleep because we don't really trust God to work it out. God says, *"Don't fear and don't fret. Remember, I'm always with you and you need to trust my timing."*

The Scripture, in our text above, says, *"Wait patiently for Him to act."* When you wait impatiently, it doesn't make the waiting any better. Your impatience is only making you more miserable, as nothing will still work, anyway! *"Don't fret and worry. It only leads to harm."*

Worry doesn't work. It just makes you miserable and panicky. So, stop worrying and start trusting God's timing.

"God has set the right time for everything." - **Ecclesiastes 3:11**
God's timing is perfect.

Chapter 23

Don't Give Up "Your Dream"

"All the Israelites grumbled against Moses...
`If only we had died in Egypt!...
We should choose a leader and go back to Egypt."
- Numbers 14:2

When you go through trials and delays in life, don't faint. Don't get discouraged. Don't lose heart. Don't give up. The Bible says:

When they gave up on their dream, they caved in. They had been in slavery for 400 years, but now because they were having a little bit of delay they wanted to go back to

Egypt. The phrases "If only" and "going back" are the tell-tale signs showing you're already discouraged, fainting, losing heart, and giving up.

> [1] *"And all the congregation lifted up their voice, and cried, and the people wept that night.*
>
> [2] *And all the children of Israel murmured against Moses and against Aaron: and the whole congregation said unto them, Would God that we had died in the land of Egypt! or would God we had died in this wilderness!*
>
> [3] *And wherefore hath the LORD brought us unto this land, to fall by the sword, that our wives and our children should be a prey? Was it not better for us to return to Egypt?*
>
> [4] *And they said one to another, Let us make a captain, and let us return into Egypt."*
>
> **- Numbers 14:1-4**

When we get a vision from God and make the decision to follow it; if it doesn't manifest immediately, we begin to doubt the vision and God's instruction about it, for which we start to look for ways to nullify it, with statements, like: "maybe I didn't hear from God; maybe I just made this up; maybe God is not listening and He doesn't care. If only I had done something different. Maybe there are some powers and demonic spirits behind the delay or maybe it is my sin or perhaps, my parents have sinned..." and the list goes on. "If only I'd done this or that..." Thereafter, we also begin to second-guess ourselves and doubt the dream.

When we go through trials and challenges or delays in our lives, we tend to bring back the past; we turn all our bad and ugly past to the good old days and we call them 'good old days' when there isn't anything good about them. The only thing good about our past trials and delays is that they're over and done with. But "Let's go back to Egypt…" you too are saying.

The good old days always look better in our sight than they really are. The Israelites had been in slavery in Egypt for 400 years and within one month of freedom, they were saying, Egypt was better. When they were in Egypt, they cried unto the Lord for deliverance; now out of Egypt, by His mighty hand, God made them face trials. Then, their story quickly changed and they began to refer to their slavery experience as the good old days and they desired to go back to it.

Some people would rather live in slavery than face the fear of freedom. They are not willing to push through and work on the problem until they get it right; they will rather complain and blame someone else for their misfortunes. They want to go back and give up. They will always settle for mediocrity in life.

Don't settle for less than God's best for your life. If that means going through a tunnel of conflict, take the tunnel.

In the middle of the tunnel, it's dark and you will want to run back to the safe light but you've got to keep going, and, trust me, you will soon come out into the light on the other side. Instead of fainting, be persistent and pray. Fight for your destiny.

> *"Let us never grow tired of doing what's right, for if we do not faint, we'll reap a harvest at the right time."*
> **- Galatians 6:9**

Jesus said this, about 2000 years earlier:

"You need to pray continually and not lose heart." **- Luke 18:1**

You have two options in life: pray and not lose heart or faint and lose heart. You will always be doing one or the other at any given time. If you pray continually, you will not lose heart or be discouraged. If you don't pray continually, you will lose your heart and faint or give up your golden dream. Don't forget that discouragement will come our way due to the problems we are facing in our lives, family, school, or wherever. So, you've got to keep on praying; you've got to keep on moving.

How should you pray during the delayed phases of life? I recommend you pray, "Lord, help me hold on and not give up." The Bible says;

> *"They that wait upon the Lord, shall renew their strength.*
> *They shall mount up with wings, as eagles.*
> *They shall run and not be weary.*
> *They shall walk and not faint."*
> **- Isaiah 40:31**

They won't give up. They'll keep on keeping on.

Victory is ahead!

Chapter 24

Bless the "Lord"

¹ "Bless the LORD, O my soul:
and all that is within me, bless his holy name;
² Bless the LORD, O my soul, and forget not all his benefits:
³ Who forgiveth all thine iniquities;
who healeth all thy diseases;
⁴ Who redeemeth thy life from destruction; who crowneth thee
with loving kindness and tender mercies;
⁵ Who satisfieth thy mouth with good things; so that thy youth
is renewed like the eagles. "
- Psalms 103:1-5

If we do not do anything about our vision at the appropriate time, due to delays and challenges, it will begin to fade away into thin air from our minds. When there are challenges beyond our expectations, we will also tend to put our dreams aside. We tend to forget what God has done in our lives and His goodness to us in the past. We even forget who God is while we also choose not to believe in His power anymore. We tend to forget how important it is that we stay in God's strength and remember what He has done for us in the past, rather than focus on all our problems. The Bible says, don't forget! Recalling the experience of the children of Israel on this and exhorting us with it, the Psalmist says:

> 7 "*Our fathers understood not thy wonders in Egypt; they remembered not the multitude of thy mercies; but provoked him at the sea, even at the Red Sea.*
>
> 8 *Nevertheless he saved them for his name's sake, that he might make his mighty power to be known.*
>
> 9 *He rebuked the Red Sea also, and it was dried up: so he led them through the depths, as through the wilderness.*
>
> 10 *And he saved them from the hand of him that hated them and redeemed them from the hand of the enemy.*
>
> 11 *And the waters covered their enemies: there was not one of them left.*
>
> 12 *Then believed they his words; they sang his praise.* 13 *They soon forgot his works; they waited not for his counsel:"*
>
> **- Psalms 106:7-13**

This was the fourth mistake that the Israelites made out in the wilderness. What exactly was the mistake? Quoting from the above Scripture, the Bible says:

> *"They forgot the many times God showed them his love, and they rebelled at the Red Sea. But He saved them as He promised"*.

Take note, this Scripture says, *'the many times'*. It's unbelievable how short their memory was. If you can remember what God did to Pharaoh in Egypt: how God terrorized the Egyptians with the ten plagues, including the killing of the firstborn male of all Egyptians but spared the children of Israel and by His mighty hand set them free from captivity; just a few days later, they were at the Red Sea, saying "We're all going to die! Let us go back to Egypt" They've forgotten the power of God they had just experienced. For their sake, God worked a miracle by opening the Red Sea; a great miracle they had never experienced in their generation, and they walked through to the other side but guess what! Immediately, they forgot that miracle too. "We're going to die of thirst!" they said again, no sooner they got into the wilderness. Then, God provided water miraculously. Nonetheless, they soon forgot about that and complained again, saying, "We're going to die, we have no food!" They were always forgetting and complaining.

We should not be too quick to judge them because we too do the exact thing. Many of us are just like them; it is so

144

easy for us to forget what God has done for us in the past. When a delay occurs in our lives, we start acting like God never did anything for us. We cry we complain, we even make the Church or the Pastor our enemy; then also, your spouse becomes the witch in your home and you too now choose to become difficult to deal with, simply because you have easily forgotten what God had done for you in the past.

Truthfully, has God done things for you in the past? Sure He has. You can count on Him to do it tomorrow, or the next day. If God has done it in the past, He can still do it again. But when you act like, "God's not going to bail me out of this one," you're forgetting all the other times He's bailed you out. There are many times when God has rescued you that you don't even know about. You only know one out of the ten times that the Lord has bailed you out.

Let me help you understand one fact today, in pure black and white, point blank: God's promises are always greater than the problems you're facing now!

> *"I will bless the Lord and not forget*
> *the great things He does for me."*
> **- Psalm 103**

You may say, "Why isn't God fulfilling His promises in my life? I have prayed, fasted, and in fact, pay my tithe regularly." Guess what! God is waiting for you while you think you're waiting for God. He's waiting for you to learn not to fear; not to fret; not to faint and not to forget. He wants you to learn that before He brings the solution, there are some things you must develop first; some growth patterns you need to put into your life.

God is never in a hurry. He can do things immediately or choose to be slow. He is the Planner and Owner of our lives and besides, our thoughts are not His own thoughts. You may think your vision is big but understand that He's working on a larger picture.

The delays that come in your life do not destroy God's purpose. They fulfill God's purpose in your life instead; the delays make you a better person. God will make a way where there seems to be no way if only we will just learn to wait.

> *"These things won't happen right away. Slowly, steadily, surely, the time approaches when the vision will be fulfilled. If it seems slow, do not despair, for these things will surely come to pass. Just be patient! They will not be overdue a single day!"*
> **- Habakkuk 2:3**

The things you've been waiting for in your life, God will bring to fulfillment if you do not faint. Do not fret, do not fear, and do not forget to always bless the Lord and recognize that He only is able to do all things according to His riches in glory.

Chapter 25

Do it All for "His Glory"

Finally, it is not a sin to be happy; your heavenly father has given you a life to be treasured and enjoyed to the fullest.

*W*hen it is filled with the spice of resonating laughter and humor, you are that much richer.

The fact is that true happiness can ease the stress and strain of life and will surely heal a confused spirit. As you continue your journey of life, live in such a way that your life is interspersed with joy and happiness.

You have every reason for great joy because God loves you, Christ died for you and the Holy Spirit leads you into many joyous paths. If you can laugh at yourself, laugh with your spouse, and children and make people around you happy; you will make this world a better place; not only for yourself but also for those around you.

Keep in mind that obedience to the Word of God will enable you to enjoy your life.

I believe strongly that, if you act on this message, you will have the most productive year in your life. Thus says the Lord, concerning you this year.

⁸ *"But thou, Israel, art my servant, Jacob whom I have chosen, the seed of Abraham my friend.*

⁹ *Thou whom I have taken from the ends of the earth, and called thee from the chief men thereof, and said unto thee, Thou art my servant; I have chosen thee, and not cast thee away.*

¹⁰ *Fear thou not; for I am with thee: be not dismayed; for I am thy God: I will strengthen thee; yea, I will help thee; yea, I will uphold thee with the right hand of my righteousness.*

¹¹ *Behold, all they that were incensed against thee shall be ashamed and confounded: they shall be as nothing, and they that strive with thee shall perish.*

¹² *Thou shalt seek them, and shalt does not find them, even them that contended with thee: they that war against thee shall be as nothing, and as a thing of naught.*

¹³ *For I the Lord thy God will hold thy right hand, saying unto thee, Fear not; I will help thee.*

> [14] *Fear not, thou worm Jacob, and ye men of Israel; I will help thee, saith the Lord, and thy redeemer, the Holy One of Israel".*
> **- Isaiah 41:8-14.**

The spiritual nuggets in this book need to be digested every day for real improvements to be seen this very year! By God's grace, you can make this year your best year yet - spiritually and physically. Shalom!

You will succeed in Jesus' name. Amen!

God Bless you,

Pastor Moses.

About the Author

Pastor Moses O. Adedipe

Pastor Moses Adedipe, is a songwriter, composer, recording, and performing artist; a playwright, author, humanitarian and community activist; also a conference and seminar speaker. He is currently the Senior Pastor of Christ Apostolic Revival Center, in Houston, Texas. He teaches and preaches the undiluted Word of God with great passion, wisdom, and anointing.

Moses Adedipe is committed to helping the neglected and the poor in the community and all over the world.

He is also the president and CEO of the African Community Emergency Response Team (www.africancert.com). He believes that "Until the poor and the neglected are reached and there is no hunger in the land, the gospel is not complete." His passion originated from the Word of God, as quoted below:

> *"Religion that God our Father accepts as pure and faultless is this: to look after orphans and widows in their distress and to keep oneself from being polluted by the world"*
> **- James 1:27**

Pastor Moses believes that, until this righteous job is completed, that is when the Christian purpose of living is truly fulfilled.

As a loving father, husband, and family man, Pastor Adedipe is married to Evangelist Catherine O. Adedipe and they are blessed with four children.

Pastor Moses Adedipe writes from a deep personal understanding of the dynamics of how to maximize your potential and fulfill your destiny. He is a minister that is in great demand at conferences and seminars, worldwide. He and his family reside in Houston, Texas, USA.

Other books by the author

The Throne of Grace - Understanding the Blessedness of the Throne of Grace

Conquering your Giant - Fear

Eviction of the Buyer: The Seller and the Money Changer

The Battle for Destiny

The King is Coming

To buy copies, please visit:

www.amazon.com

www.cacbibleinstitude.org

www.campofgod.org

Please, contact Pastor Moses Adedipe @

7623 Drifting Willow Court. Cypress. Texas 77433

Phone: 281-804-2520,

281-324-0060,

281-769-7100

arewamose@att.net

cacrevivalcenter@gmail.com

www.cacrevivalcenter.org,

www.mosesadedipe.com

Publishers:

Mercyland Publishing House (MPH)

Mercyland Inc- (www.mercylandinc.com)